ON THE TRACK.

THE   DEPARTURE

ON THE TRACK.

BY

JULES VERNE,

AUTHOR OF "A JOURNEY INTO THE INTERIOR OF THE EARTH,"
"THE ENGLISH AT THE NORTH POLE," ETC. ETC.

Fredonia Books
Amsterdam, The Netherlands

On the Track

by
Jules Verne

ISBN: 1-58963-491-8

Reprinted from the original edition

Fredonia Books
Amsterdam, The Netherlands
http://www.fredoniabooks.com

CONTENTS.

Contents.

ON THE TRACK.

CHAPTER I.

ON BOARD THE DUNCAN.

OR the benefit of those readers who may not have read "The Mysterious Document," of which this is a sequel, we must introduce our characters, and state where they are, and why they are there, when our story opens.

Lord Glenarvan, a Scotch nobleman, and his wife, Lady Helena Glenarvan, Mary Grant, and her young brother Robert, Major MacNabbs, cousin of the Glenarvans, an absent-minded French savant, Paganel by name, Captain John Mangles, and a ship's crew, are all on board the Duncan, a steam yacht belonging to Lord Glenarvan.

The Duncan lies at anchor off the coast of the Argentine Republic, whence Lord Glenarvan, Paganel, the major, Robert Grant, and two sailors have just embarked. These six men have followed the 37th parallel of austral latitude right across South America. They undertook the journey in search of Captain Grant,

Robert's father, who, with two sailors, was wrecked in the ship Britannia two years before our story opens, and has never since been heard of.

The only indications the travellers had to go upon were furnished by a half-obliterated document, written in English, French, and German, found in a bottle in the Firth of Clyde by the crew of the Duncan. The following conversation, which took place in the saloon cabin, will, with the tale, explain the rest.

"When we came back on board, dear Helena," said Lord Glenarvan to his young wife, "I told you that, although we had not brought the shipwrecked men from the Britannia back with us, we have more than ever the hope of finding them eventually. From our passage across America this conviction has resulted, that the catastrophe neither took place on the shores of the Pacific nor the Atlantic. Happily, our friend Paganel, illuminated by a sudden inspiration, has discovered our error. He has demonstrated that we have been following a false track, and has so interpreted the document found in the bottle as to leave no doubt in our minds. The document written in French has been freshly interpreted by Paganel, and he will read it to you."

Paganel took the yellow piece of paper, upon which only a few syllables remained, and, filling up the spaces, read it as follows :—

"On the 7th of June, 1862, the ship Britannia, of Glasgow, went down, after a long agony, on the coasts of Australia. Captain Grant and two sailors landed on the continent, where they are prisoners of cruel natives. They threw this document by longitude —— and latitude 37° 11'."

When Paganel had read the document, and explained why he interpreted it thus, Glenarvan announced that the Duncan should immediately set sail for Australia. However, before the order was given, Major Mac-Nabbs asked to be allowed to make a simple observation.

"Speak, MacNabbs," answered Glenarvan.

"My wish," said the major, "is not to weaken the arguments of my friend Paganel, still less to refute them; I find them serious, wise, and worthy of all our attention, and they ought to form the basis of our future search. But I desire that they may be submitted to further examination, in order that their value may be indisputable and undisputed."

None knew what the prudent MacNabbs was coming to, and his auditors listened to him in some anxiety.

"Go on, major," said Paganel. "I am ready to answer all your questions."

"When, five months ago," continued the major, "we studied the three documents in the Firth of Clyde, their interpretation appeared to us evident. No other than the eastern coast of Patagonia could have been the theatre of the shipwreck. We had not even the shadow of a doubt on the subject."

"That is true," answered Glenarvan.

"Later on," continued the major, "when Paganel, in a moment of providential distraction, came on board, the documents were submitted to him, and he approved, without reserve, of our search on the American continent."

"I acknowledge it," answered the geographer.

"And yet we were all mistaken," said the major.

"Yes, we were mistaken," answered Paganel. "But

men are allowed mistakes, they are only fools who persist in them."

"Wait a minute, Paganel," said the major, "and do not excite yourself. I do not mean that we ought to continue our search in America."

"Then what do you want?" asked Glenarvan.

"The acknowledgment, nothing more, that Australia now appears to be the theatre of the shipwreck of the Britannia on as good grounds as America seemed formerly."

"We readily acknowledge it," answered Paganel.

"And I make a note of it," answered the major, "and profit by it to ask you not to believe too readily these successive and contradictory evidences. Who knows if, after Australia, another country will not offer you the same certainty? And if, after a fresh search made in vain, it will not seem to you ' evident' that we ought to begin again elsewhere?"

Glenarvan and Paganel looked at one another. The major's observations struck them by their justice.

"I desire, then," continued MacNabbs, "to have a map of the countries through which the 37th parallel runs, and to see if there does not exist some other country which the document will indicate precisely."

"Nothing could be easier or quicker to do," answered Paganel, "for, happily, land does not abound under that latitude."

The major unfolded an English planisphere, according to Mercator's projection, which showed the whole terrestrial globe. The map was placed before Lady Glenarvan, and they all placed themselves so as to follow Paganel's demonstration.

"As you see," said the geographer, " after crossing

South America, the 37th degree of latitude passes the Tristan d'Acunha Islands. Now I affirm that not one word in the document can refer to these islands."

The documents were scrupulously examined, and they all acknowledged that Paganel was right. Tristan d'Acunha was rejected unanimously.

"Getting out of the Atlantic," continued the geographer, "we pass two degrees below the Cape of Good Hope, and penetrate into the Indian Ocean. One single group of islands is on our route, the Amsterdam Islands. Submit them to the same examination as the Tristan d'Acunha Islands."

After an attentive scrutiny, the Amsterdam Islands were also rejected. No word, or portion of a word, in French, English, or German, could apply to this group in the Indian Ocean.

"Now we arrive at Australia," continued Paganel; "the 37th parallel meets this continent at Cape Bernouilli, and leaves it in Twofold Bay. You will agree with me that the word *stra* in the English document, and *austral* in the French, may apply to Australia. The thing is too evident to be insisted upon."

They all agreed with Paganel's conclusion.

"Let us go beyond," said the major.

"The journey is easy," answered the geographer. "Leaving Twofold Bay we cross the sea at the east of Australia, and meet with New Zealand. I must remind you that the word *contin* in the French document certainly indicates a continent, and New Zealand is only an island. However that may be, examine, compare, and see if the indications can bear upon this new country."

"In no wise," answered John Mangles, who made a

minute examination of the documents and the plani-sphere.

"No," said Paganel's audience, and the major him-self, "no, there can be no question of New Zealand."

"Now," continued the geographer, "on all this immense space, which separates New Zealand from the American coast, the 37th parallel only crosses one arid and desert islet."

"Called?" asked the major.

"See the map. It is the Maria Theresa, a name of which I do not find the slightest trace in either of the three documents."

"There is none," answered Glenarvan. "I leave you then to decide if all these probabilities, not to say certainties, are not in favour of the Australian continent."

The passengers and captain of the Duncan agreed that they did.

"Captain," then said Glenarvan, "have you a suffi-cient quantity of provisions and coal?"

"Yes, my lord. I laid in a good stock at Talca-huano; and besides, we can touch at Cape Town for coal."

"Will you allow me to make another observation?" said the major to Glenarvan.

"As many as you please, major."

"Don't you think it would be wise to touch at the Tristan d'Acunha and Amsterdam Islands for a few days? We should then find out if the Britannia has left any trace of her shipwreck there."

"Incredulous major," cried Paganel.

"I do not want us to have to retrace our steps, if Australia should not realise our hopes."

"The precaution seems to me good," answered Glenarvan.

"And I shall certainly not dissuade you from taking it," said Paganel; "on the contrary."

"Then, John," said Glenarvan, "make for the Tristan d'Acunha Islands."

"This instant, my lord," answered the captain, and he went up on deck, whilst Mary and Robert Grant tried to thank their benefactor.

The Duncan was soon sailing away from the American coast, and cutting, with her rapid prow, the waves of the Atlantic Ocean.

CHAPTER II.

TRISTAN D'ACUNHA.

IF the yacht had followed the equatorial line, the 196° which separate Australia from America, or Cape Bernouilli from Cape Corrientes, she would have had 11,760 geographical miles to go. But on the 37th parallel, on account of the form of the globe, the distance was only 9,480 miles. From the American coast to Tristan d'Acunha it is 2,100 miles, a distance which John Mangles hoped to clear in ten days, if the east winds did not retard the ship. That very evening the wind lulled perceptibly, then changed, and the Duncan could display all her incomparable qualities on a tranquil sea.

The passengers had taken up again their usual life on board. After the waves of the Pacific those of the

Atlantic lay stretched before them, and, with the exception of different shades, all waves are very much alike. The rapid passage was accomplished without accident or incident. Probabilities changed to certainties in the minds of the passengers. They talked of Captain Grant as if the yacht were to take him up in some port agreed upon. His cabin was prepared on board. It pleased Mary Grant to prepare and embellish it herself.

The learned geographer kept himself almost constantly shut up. He worked night and day at a book he was writing, entitled " Sublime Impressions of a Geographer in the Argentine Prairies." They heard him read aloud his elegant periods before confiding them to the blank pages of his memorandum book, and more than once, faithless to Clio, the muse of history, he involved in his transports divine Calliope, who presides over epic works. He did not hide his light under a bushel either, and Lady Glenarvan paid him her sincerest compliments. The major congratulated him on his mythological visitors.

" But no absence of mind, Paganel!" he added. " If the fancy takes you to learn Australian, don't study it in a Chinese grammar."

This speech referred to the absent-minded savant having learnt Portuguese when he thought he was learning Spanish.

Lord and Lady Glenarvan watched John Mangles and Mary Grant with interest. They saw nothing they could object to, and decidedly, as John did not speak, it was better to take no notice.

" What will Captain Grant think of it?" said Glenarvan one day to his wife.

"He will think that John is worthy of Mary, Edward, and he will not be mistaken."

In the meantime the yacht was marching rapidly towards her destination. Five days after losing sight of Cape Corrientes, on the 16th of November, the wind sprang up in the west, the very wind which is so convenient for ships doubling the Cape of Good Hope against the regular winds from the south-east. The captain put all sail on, and the yacht flew along as if she were running one of the Royal Thames Club races.

The next day the ocean looked like a vast pond, choked up with herbs. The Duncan appeared to glide over a long prairie, which Paganel justly compared to the Pampas, and its course was a little delayed. Twenty-four hours afterwards, at daybreak, the man at the mast-head called out—

"Land a-head!"

At this cry, always agitating, the deck was immediately filled with people. Soon a telescope issued from the companion-ladder, and was followed by Jacques Paganel. The savant pointed his telescope in the direction indicated, and saw nothing resembling land.

"Look in the clouds," said Mangles to him.

"I see now," answered Paganel, "it looks like a sort of peak, still imperceptible."

"That is Tristan d'Acunha," cried Mangles.

"Then, if I remember rightly," replied the savant, "we must be eighty miles away from it, for the peak of Tristan, 7,000 feet high, is visible at that distance."

"Precisely," answered Mangles.

A few hours later, the group of very high and very steep islands was perfectly visible on the horizon. The

B

conical peak of Tristan stood out black against a sky
all striped with the rays of the rising sun. Soon the
principal island emerged from the rocky mass at the
summit of a triangle, inclined towards the N.E.

Tristan d'Acunha is situated in longitude 10° 44′ by
south latitude 37° 8′. Eighteen miles to the S.W.,
Inaccessible Island, and ten miles to the S.E., Nightingale Island, complete the little group lying all alone
in this part of the Atlantic. About noon they sighted
the two principal landmarks by which sailors know
this group : a rock looking exactly like a boat under sail,
at an angle with Inaccessible Island, and the northern
point of Nightingale Island, two islets like a ruined
fortress. At three o'clock the Duncan was entering the
Falmouth Bay of Tristan d'Acunha, which Help Point
shelters from the west winds. There some whalers lay
at anchor, occupied in fishing seals and other marine
animals, of which these coasts offer numerous specimens.
Mangles looked out for a good place to anchor in, for
these roadsteads are very dangerous in north-westerly
and north gales, and it was precisely in this place that
the English brig Julia was lost in 1829. The Duncan
approached to within half a mile of the shore, and
anchored in twenty fathoms on a foundation of rocks.
The passengers immediately embarked in the long boat,
and set foot on fine black sand, the impalpable remains
of calcined rocks.

The capital of the group is a little village situated on
the bay, near a murmuring stream. There were about
fifty houses, pretty, clean, and placed in that geometrical
regularity that appears to be the last word of English
architecture. Behind this town in miniature extends
1,500 acres of plains, bordered by an immense embank-

ment of lava; above this plateau the conical peak rose 7,000 feet into the air.

Lord Glenarvan was received by a governor who is sent out by Cape Colony. He immediately inquired about Captain Grant and the Britannia. Their names were entirely unknown. The Tristan d'Acunha Islands are out of the way of ships, and very little frequented in consequence. Since the celebrated shipwreck of the Blendon Hall, which foundered, in 1821, on the rocks of Inaccessible Island, two ships had been wrecked in the principal island, the Primauguet in 1845, and the American ship Philadelphia in 1857. Glenarvan did not expect to receive more precise information, and only questioned the governor as a duty. He even sent his boats round the island, the circumference of which is seventeen miles. Neither London nor Paris could stand upon it, even were it three times as large. In the meantime the passengers of the Duncan walked about the town and neighbourhood. The population of Tristan d'Acunha does not reach 150 inhabitants. They are English or Americans, married to Cape Hottentots, who leave nothing to be desired in the matter of ugliness. The children of the heterogeneous marriages present a very disagreeable mixture of Saxon stiffness and African blackness.

This tourist's walk was prolonged along the shore, touched by the large cultivated plain which only exists in that part of the island. Everywhere else the coast is made of lava cliffs, arid and steep. There were enormous albatros and stupid penguins by hundreds of thousands.

The visitors, after having examined those volcanic rocks, climbed them towards the plain; numerous and lively streams, fed by the eternal snows of the cone, murmured here and there; green bushes, on which the eye could count as many sparrows as flowers, made the soil grey; a single tree, a sort of "phylique," twenty feet high, and the "tussek," a gigantic plant, aromatic and balsamic plants, loaded the breeze with penetrating odours; mosses, wild celery, and ferns made up an opulent but restricted flora. It was evident that eternal spring poured its gentle influence on this privileged island. Paganel, with his habitual enthusiasm, maintained that it was the famous Ogygie spoken of by Fénélon. He proposed to Lady Glenarvan to look for a grotto, so that she might succeed the amiable Calypso, and asked for no other employment for himself than to be "one of her attendant nymphs."

It was thus that, talking and admiring, the party returned to the yacht at nightfall; around the village oxen and sheep were pasturing; fields of wheat, maize, and vegetables, imported during the last forty years, came right up to the streets of the capital.

Lord Glenarvan went back on board as the boats returned to the yacht. They had only taken a few hours to go round the island. They had met with no trace of the Britannia, and this voyage of circumnavigation had no other result than that of eliminating definitely the island of Tristan from the programme of places to search.

The Duncan could then leave this group of African islands and continue her route eastward. She did not start the same evening, because Glenarvan authorised his crew to give chase to the innumerable seals which, under the name of calves, lions, bears, and marine elephants, encumbered the shores of Falmouth Bay.

Formerly, whales sported in the waters of the island; but they had been so much hunted by the whalers that there were scarcely any left. Amphibians were there in flocks. The yacht's crew resolved to employ the night in hunting them, and the following day in making an ample provision of oil. The departure of the Duncan was, therefore, put off till November 30th.

During supper, Paganel gave some details about the Tristan Islands, which interested his hearers. They learnt that this group, discovered in 1506 by the Portuguese Tristan d'Acunha, one of the companions of Albuquerque, remained unexplored for more than a century. These islands passed, not without reason, as nests for tempests, and had no better reputation than the Bermudas. They were, therefore, very seldom approached, and no ship ever anchored there that was not thrown on to them by the Atlantic hurricanes. In 1697 the Dutch ships of the East India Company put in there and made out their configuration, leaving to the great astronomer, Halley, the care of revising their calculations in the year 1700. From 1712 to 1767, some French navigators made acquaintance with them, and principally La Perouse, whose instructions carried him there during his celebrated voyage in 1785.

These islands, till then so little visited, were still unpeopled, when, in 1811, an American, Jonathan Lambert, undertook to colonise them. He and his companions landed there in the month of January, and did courageously their trade of colonists. The English governor at the Cape, having learnt that they were prospering, offered them the protection of England. Johnson accepted, and hoisted the British

flag over his cabin. He seemed to have reigned peacefully over his people, composed of an old Indian and a
Portuguese mulatto, when one day, whilst reconnoitring the shores of his empire, he drowned himself,
or was drowned, it is not well known which. 1816
arrived. Napoleon was imprisoned at Saint Helena,
and, in order to guard him better, England established
a garrison on Ascension Island, and another at Tristan
d'Acunha. The garrison of Tristan consisted of a
company of artillery from the Cape and a detachment
of Hottentots. It remained there until 1821, and, on
the death of the prisoner of Saint Helena, it was sent
back to the Cape.

"One single European," added Paganel, "a Scotch
corporal——"

"Ah! a Scotchman!" said the major, whom his
countrymen interested particularly.

"He was named William Glass," answered Paganel,
"and he remained in the island with his wife and two
Hottentots. Soon two Englishmen, a sailor and a
Thames waterman, ex-dragoon in the Argentine army,
joined the Scotchman, and at last, in 1821, one of the
men shipwrecked in the Blendon Hall, and accompanied by his young wife, took refuge in Tristan Island.
Thus then, in 1821, the island contained six men and
two women. In 1829 there were seven men, six women,
and fourteen children. In 1835, there were forty ; and
now there are three times as many."

"That is how nations begin," said Glenarvan.

"I must add," continued Paganel, "in order to
complete the history of Tristan d'Acunha, that this
island appears to me to deserve the name of Crusoe
Island as much as that of Juan Fernandez. Two

sailors were successively abandoned at Juan Fernandez, and two savants were very nearly being so at Tristan d'Acunha. In 1793, one of my countrymen, the naturalist, Aubert Dupetit-Thouars, carried away by his ardour for botanising, got lost, and could not rejoin his ship before the captain was raising the anchor. In 1824, one of your countrymen, Glenárvan, a clever draughtsman, Augustus Earle, remained for eight months abandoned in the island. His captain, forgetting that he was on land, had set sail for the Cape."

"That is what might be called an absent-minded captain," answered the major. "One of your relations, no doubt, Paganel."

"If he was not, major, he deserved to be."

This answer of the geographer terminated the conversation.

During the night the crew of the Duncan killed fifty fat seals. After having authorised the killing, Glenarvan could not interdict the profit. The following day was, therefore, employed in making the oil and preparing the skins of these lucrative amphibians. The passengers naturally employed this second day in making another excursion in the island. Glenarvan and the major took their guns to try the Acunhian game. During their walk, they went to the foot of the mountain, on a soil covered with volcanic remains. Captain Carmichael was right in considering it an extinct volcano.

The hunters perceived several wild boars. One of them fell, struck by a bullet from the major. Glenarvan was contented with bringing down several couples of black partridges, of which the cook would make a delicious dish. A great quantity of goats was seen on the summits of elevated plateaux. As to the wild cats, they were formidable, even to the dogs, and they promised one day to become very distinguished wild beasts.

At eight p.m. everybody was back on board, and in the night the Duncan left Tristan d'Acunha, to see it no more.

CHAPTER III.

AMSTERDAM ISLAND.

T was John Mangles' intention to go to Cape Town for coal. He was, therefore, obliged to sail a little out of his route along the 37th parallel, and go two degrees farther north. The Duncan was then below the zone of the trade-winds, and met with west winds very favourable for her passage. In less than six days she cleared the 1,300 miles which separated Tristan d'Acunha from the Cape of Good Hope. On the 24th of November, at three p.m., Table Mountain was sighted, and afterwards Signal Mountain, at the entrance of the bay. At eight p.m. Mangles anchored in the port of Cape Town.

Paganel, in his quality of member of the Geographical Society, could not ignore that the extremity of Africa was seen for the first time in 1486 by the Portuguese Admiral Bartholomew Diaz, and only doubled in 1497 by the celebrated Vasco de Gama. And how could Paganel be ignorant of it, when Camoëns had sung the glory of the great navigator in his *Lusiad?* But upon this subject he made a curious observation—viz., that if Diaz, in 1486, had doubled the Cape of Good Hope, the discovery of America was put off indefinitely. In fact, the route by the Cape was the shortest and most direct to the East Indies, and the great Genevese navigator only went westward to try and abridge the route to the spice country. Therefore, the Cape once doubled, he would have had no motive for his expedition, and would probably never have undertaken it.

Cape Town, situated upon Cape Bay, was founded in 1652 by the Dutchman Van Riebeck. It was the capital of an important colony, which became decidedly English after the treaties of 1815. The passengers of the Duncan had twelve hours in which to make its acquaintance, for one day sufficed Mangles to renew his provisions, and he wished to start again early on the morning of the 26th.

No more time was necessary to go over the regular streets of the chess-board called Cape Town, on which 30,000 white and black inhabitants play their parts. When the castle, which rises in the south-east of the town, the government-house and garden, the exchange, the museum, and the stone cross raised there by Diaz at the time of his discovery, have all been seen, and a glass of "Pontai" made from the first growth of the Constance grape had been drunk, there is nothing to do but depart, and that is what the travellers did at daybreak the next morning. In a few hours the Duncan doubled the famous Cape of Tempests, to which the optimist King of Portugal, John II., unfortunately gave the name of Good Hope.

There were 2,900 miles to clear between the Cape and Amsterdam Island. If the wind and sea were favourable, it would be the affair of ten days. The navigators had no cause to complain of the elements.

"Ah! the sea! the sea!" exclaimed Paganel. "Think of what we owe it. If the globe had only been an immense continent, not the thousandth part of it would be known in the nineteenth century. See what happens in the interior of great continents. In the steppes of Siberia, in the plains of Central Asia, the deserts of Africa, the prairies of America, the vast lands of Australia, the glacial solitudes of the poles, men dare scarcely venture, the boldest draw back, the most courageous succumb. Twenty miles of desert separate men more effectually than 500 miles of ocean. People are neighbours from one coast to another; strangers if separated only by a forest. England is near Australia, whilst Egypt seems to be millions of miles from Senegal and Pekin, the antipodes of Saint Petersburg. The sea now-a-days is crossed more easily than the least sahara; and it is thanks to the sea, as an American savant has justly said, that universal relationship has been established between all parts of the world."

Paganel spoke with warmth, and even the major himself did not find fault with a word in this panegyric of the ocean. If, to find Captain Grant, it had been necessary to follow the 37th parallel across a continent, the enterprise would not have been attempted; but the sea was there to transport the courageous seekers from one land to another, and on the 6th of September, at break of day, it let a new mountain emerge from its waves.

It was Amsterdam Island, situated in longitude 77° 24′ and latitude 37° 47′: in clear weather its elevated peak is visible fifty miles off. At eight o'clock the form of it looked like the peak of Teneriffe.

"And, consequently, it resembles Tristan d'Acunha."

"Justly concluded," answered Paganel, "according to the geometrical axiom, that two islands that are like a third are like each other. I may add that, like Tristan d'Acunha, Amsterdam Island is rich in seals and Crusoes."

"There are Crusoes everywhere, then?" asked Lady Glenarvan.

"I know very few islands that have not had adventures of the kind, and your Defoe's novel had often been enacted before he wrote it."

"Mr. Paganel," said Mary Grant, "will you allow me to ask you a question?"

"Two if you like, and I promise to answer them."

"Would you be very much frightened at the idea of being abandoned on a desert island?"

"Come, Paganel," said the major, "are you not going to acknowledge that it is your dearest wish?"

"No, I will not acknowledge that," replied the geographer; "yet I should not dislike the adventure. I would make a fresh life for myself. I should hunt and fish, live in a cave in the winter, on a tree in the summer; I should have store-houses for my grain, and, in short, I should colonise my island."

"What, all by yourself?"

"Yes, all by myself, were it necessary. Besides, I could tame animals—a young kid, an eloquent parrot, or an amiable monkey. And if accident sent me a companion like the faithful Friday, what more could I desire to make me happy? Suppose the major and I——"

" Thanks," answered the major, " I have no desire to play the part of a Crusoe, and should do it very badly."

" Your imagination is running away with you again, M. Paganel," said Lady Glenarvan ; " but I believe the reality is something very different. You only think of imaginary Crusoes, carefully thrown upon a well-selected island. You only see the bright side of things."

" Do not you think it possible to be happy in a desert island, then ?"

" No, I do not. Man is made for society, not isolation. Solitude can only engender despair. It is possible that the necessity for thinking of the material things of life should distract the unhappy man at first. But afterwards, when he realises the extent of his solitude, he must suffer torments."

Paganel gave in, not without regret, to Lady Glenarvan's arguments, and the conversation on the relative advantages of solitude and society went on till the Duncan anchored at one mile from the shore of Amsterdam Island. This group, isolated in the Indian Ocean, is formed of two distinct islands at about thirty-three miles from one another, and precisely on the meridian of the Indian peninsula ; the island on the north is Amsterdam, or Saint Peter, and the one on the south Saint Paul ; but they have often been mistaken for one another by geographers and navigators.

These islands were discovered in December, 1796, by the Dutchman Vlaming, then recognised by Entre-casteaux, who took the Espérance and the Recherche in search of La Pérouse. In 1859 the officers on board the Austrian frigate Novara, in her voyage of circum-navigation, avoided committing the error of mistaking the two islands, and Paganel much wished to rectify it. Saint Paul, situated to the south of Amsterdam Island, is only an uninhabited islet, formed of a conical mountain, which must have been formerly a volcano. Amsterdam Island, to which the yacht was rapidly bearing her passengers, is about twelve miles in circumference. It is inhabited by voluntary exiles, who have grown accustomed to their dull existence. These are the guardians of the fishery, which belongs, as does the island, to a certain M. Otovan, merchant of the Reunion. This sovereign, who is not yet acknowledged by the great European Powers, makes a civil list of about £3,000 by fishing, salting, and exporting a "cheilodactylus," known less scientifically under the name of salt cod.

This island was destined to become and remain French. In fact, it first of all belonged, by right of first occupant, to M. Carmin, captain of a privateer from Saint Denis to Bourbon; then it was ceded, in virtue of some international contract, to a Pole, who had it cultivated by slaves. Then the island became French again in the hands of M. Otovan.

When the Duncan accosted it on the 6th of December, 1864, its population numbered three inhabitants—one Frenchman and two mulattos, all three clerks of the merchant-proprietor. Paganel could, therefore, shake hands with a countryman in the person of M. Viot, then an extremely old man. This patriarch did the honours of his island with much politeness. It was a happy day for him, as Saint Peter is only frequented by seal-fishers or whalers. He presented his subjects, the two mulattos; they formed the living population of the island. Their little house was situated on a natural

port to the S.W., formed by the falling down of a part
of the mountain.

M. Viot had heard of no shipwreck, nor seen any
traces of one. Glenarvan was neither surprised nor
saddened by his answer. He wished to be certain that
Captain Grant was not there, but he had not the least
expectation of finding him there. The departure of the
Duncan was, therefore, fixed for the next day. Until evening the passengers went about the island, which has a
very attractive appearance; but neither its fauna nor
flora would have filled the octavo of the most prolix of
naturalists. A few wild boars, petrels, albatros, perches,
and seals, comprised the live stock. Thermal waters
and ferruginous springs escaped, here and there, from
the blackish waters, and threw their thick vapours above
the volcanic soil. Some of these springs had a very
high temperature. Mangles plunged a Fahrenheit
thermometer into one which registered 176°. Fish
taken in the sea a few paces from the spring were cooked
in it in five minutes, which circumstance decided Paganel
not to bathe in it.

Towards evening, after a good walk, Glenarvan bade
adieu to M. Viot. Every one wished him the greatest
happiness possible on his desert islet, and he wished all
success to the expedition. Thereupon the passengers
embarked.

CHAPTER IV.

BETS.

N December 7th, at three a.m , the Duncan set sail again, and when the passengers came up on deck at eight o'clock, Amsterdam Island was disappearing on the horizon. Three thousand miles separated it from the Australian coast. If the west wind would hold on for another twelve days, the Duncan would reach her destination.

Mangles pointed out to Mary Grant the different currents shown in the maps on board, and explained their constant direction to her. One amongst them, that which crosses the Indian Ocean, bears upon the Australian continent, and its action from west to east is felt in the Pacific no less than in the Atlantic. If the Britannia had been stripped of her masts and rudder—that is to say, disarmed against the violence of sea and sky—she must have run upon the coast there.

However, one difficulty presented itself here. The last news of Captain Grant came from Callao, May 30th, 1862, according to the *Mercantile and Shipping Gazette.* How could the Britannia be in the Indian Ocean on the 7th of June, only a week after leaving the coast of Peru? This difficulty was raised one day when all the passengers were on the poop. Paganel went immediately to examine the document, and when he came back shrugged his shoulders.

"Well, Paganel, will you answer that objection?" asked Glenarvan.

"No," answered Paganel; "I shall only ask one question of Captain Mangles here. Can a good ship go along our route from America to Australia in a month?"

"Yes, if she makes 200 miles in twenty-four hours."

"Is that speed extraordinary?"

"No; clippers often go faster than that."

"Well," continued Paganel, "instead of reading June 7th on the document, let us suppose that the sea has obliterated one figure, and read 'June 17th or 27th.' From May 31st to June 27th, Captain Grant might have reached the Indian Ocean."

This conclusion of Paganel's was received with much satisfaction.

"Another point cleared up," said Glenarvan, "and thanks to our friend. Now we have only to seek traces of the Britannia on the west coast of Australia."

"Or on the east coast," said Mangles.

"Yes, you are right, John. Nothing in the document indicates whether the catastrophe occurred on the western shores rather than on the eastern."

"If Captain Grant was wrecked on the eastern shores of Australia," said John Mangles, "he would have found succour and assistance almost immediately. All the shore is English, and peopled with colonies. The crew of the Britannia had not ten miles to go before meeting with countrymen."

"Yes, captain," said Paganel. "At Twofold Bay and Eden Town, on the eastern coast, Captain Grant would not only have received shelter in an English colony, but would also have found means of transport to Europe."

"Then," said Lady Glenarvan, "the shipwrecked

men would not have found the same help on that
part of Australia to which the Duncan is taking
us ?"

" No," answered Paganel, " it is a desert coast, and
there is no communication between it and Melbourne
or Adelaide. If the Britannia was wrecked on its
breakers, all succour would have failed her as effectually as upon the inhospitable shores of Africa."

"But what can have become of my father for the
last two years ?" said Mary Grant.

" He has either reached the English colonies or
fallen into the hands of the natives, or has lost himself
in the vast solitudes of Australia. If he had reached
the English colonies, he would also have reached the
good town of Dundee long ago; so he must either be
a prisoner of the natives or——"

" But what sort of people are these natives ?" asked
Lady Glenarvan.

" They are the lowest type of humanity," answered
the savant ; " but they are not sanguinary like their
New Zealand neighbours. If they have made the captain and his sailors prisoners, they have not menaced
their existence, you may rest assured of that. All
travellers are unanimous in saying that the Australians
have a horror of bloodshed, and have many times found
them faithful allies against much more cruel bands of
convicts."

" You hear what M. Paganel says, Mary ?" said Lady
Glenarvan, turning to the young girl. " If your
father is in the hands of the natives, we shall find him
again."

"And if he is lost in that immense country ?" said
Mary, looking to Paganel for an answer.

c

"Well," cried the geographer in a confident tone, "we shall still find him. Shall we not, my friends?"

"Certainly," answered Glenarvan, who wished to give a tone less sad to the conversation. "I do not admit the possibility of being lost."

"Nor I either," replied Paganel.

"Is Australia large?" asked Robert.

"It is about as large as four-fifths of Europe, my boy; but, although it is large enough to be called a continent, very few travellers have been lost there. I believe Leichardt is the only one whose fate is unknown, and I was informed through the Geographical Society, some time before my departure, that MacIntyre believed himself to be on his track."

"Is not the whole of Australia known, then?" asked Lady Glenarvan.

"Oh no, not by a great deal," answered Paganel. "This continent is not known any better than the interior of Africa, but not for want of enterprising travellers. From 1606 to 1862 more than fifty men have worked at Australian discoveries, both on the coast and in the interior."

"Fifty!" cried the major, doubtfully.

"Yes, quite as many as that, major. I mean sailors who have discovered the outlines of the coast as well as travellers who have journeyed into the interior."

"Even then fifty is a large number."

"I will even say more, MacNabbs," continued the geographer, who was always excited by contradiction. "If you challenge me, I will quote fifty names without hesitating. Will you bet me your Purdey, Moore, and Dickson rifle against my Secretan telescope?"

"Why not, Paganel, if that can give you any pleasure?" answered MacNabbs.

"Then, major, you will kill no more chamois or foxes with that rifle unless I lend it to you, which I shall always have much pleasure in doing."

"Paganel," answered the major, seriously, "when you want my telescope, it will always be at your disposition."

"I will begin, then," said Paganel. "Ladies and gentlemen, you must be the audience, and Robert, you must count the names. Two hundred and fifty-eight years ago, my friends, Australia was still unknown. The existence of a large southern continent was suspected, and two maps kept in the library of your British Museum, dated 1550, mention a land to the south of Asia, which they call the Great Java of the Portuguese. But these maps are not sufficiently authentic. In 1606, a Spanish navigator, Quiros, discovered a land which he called Australia de Espiritu Santo. Some authors have pretended that he meant the group of the New Hebrides, and not Australia. I shall not discuss the question. Count Quiros, Robert, and I will go on to another."

"One," said Robert.

"In the same year, Luiz Vaz de Torres, who was second commander in Quiros's fleet, went further south on the new land. But it was the Dutchman, Theodoric Hertoge, to whom all the honour of the great discovery belongs. After him came many navigators. Zeachen in 1618, Jan Edels in 1619, Leuwin in 1622, Mutz and De Witt in 1627; they were followed by Carpenter and Tasman, who, in 1642, discovered Tasmania. Then the Australian continent had been sailed round; and in 1665

the name of New Holland, which it was not to keep,
was given to the large southern island at the precise
epoch that the role of its navigators ended. What
number are we at now?"

"Ten," answered Robert.

"I am now come to Englishmen," said Paganel.
"In 1686, William Dampier, the celebrated bucanier,
arrived on the N.W. coast of New Zealand, by latitude
16° 50'; he communicated with the natives, and described
them.   After a long lapse of time came the greatest
navigator of the entire world, Captain Cook, in 1770, and
after that emigrants from Europe.   He gave its name to
Botany Bay, because he found its shores so rich in new
plants.   It was his companion Banks who first sug-
gested to the English Government the idea of sending
convicts there.   After Cook came navigators from all
nations. La Pérouse wrote from Botany Bay in 1787, and
was never heard of afterwards. In 1788 Captain Philipps
established the first English colony at Port Jackson.
In 1791 Vancouver, in 1792 Entrecasteaux, in search
of La Pérouse; in 1795 and 1797 Flinders and Bass
helped to survey the new land; Vlaming, the discoverer
of Amsterdam Island in 1797; Flanders in 1801, who
met in Encounter Bay two French vessels, commanded
by Baudin and Hamelin——"

"Captain Baudin?" said the major.

"Yes, why?"

"Oh, nothing; go on."

"Then there was Captain King, from 1817 to
1822."

"That makes twenty-four names," said Robert.

"Good; I have half the major's rifle already. And
now I have done with sailors, and pass to travellers."

" What an astonishing memory you have, Mr. Paganel!" exclaimed Lady Glenarvan.

" It is very singular in a man so——"

"Absent-minded, major? Yes, I only remember dates and facts."

" Twenty-four," repeated Robert.

" Well, the twenty-fifth is Lieutenant Daws. In 1789, a year after Port Jackson was colonised, he went a nine days' march into the interior. The same year Captain Tench tried to cross the high chain of mountains, which seem a barrier to interdict the interior to travellers from the east coast, but could not succeed. In 1792, Colonel Paterson, a bold African explorer, failed in the same attempt. The following year, a simple quartermaster in the English navy passed twenty miles beyond the barrier. For the next eighteen years I have only two names to quote—Bass and M. Bareiller, an engineer from the colony, who were not more fortunate than their predecessors; and I arrive at the year 1813, when a pass was at length discovered to the west of Sydney. Governor Macquarie ventured through it in 1815, and the town of Bathurst was founded beyond the Blue Mountains. The next names are Throsby in 1819, Oxley, who journeyed over 300 miles of country, Howel and Hune, whose point of departure was precisely Twofold Bay, on the 37th parallel, and Captain Sturt, in 1829 and 1830."

" That makes thirty-six," said Robert.

"Then came Eyre and Leichardt in 1840 and 1841, Sturt in 1845, the brothers Gregory and Helpman in 1846 in Western Australia, Kennedy in 1847 on the Victoria river, and in 1848 in Northern Australia, Gregory in 1852, Austin in 1854, the Gregories from

1855 to 1858 in the N.W. of the continent, Babbage
from Lake Torrens to Lake Eyre, and I arrive, at last,
to Stuart, who went three journeys across the continent.
From 1860 to 1862 there were the brothers Dempster,
Clarkson, Harper, Burke, Wills, Neilson, Walker,
Landsborough, Mackinlay, Howit——"

"Fifty-six!" cried Robert.

"I give you good measure, major," said Paganel,
"for I have quoted neither Duperrey, nor Bougainville,
nor FitzRoy, nor Wickam, nor Stokes——"

"Hold, enough!" cried the major, overwhelmed.

"Nor Pérou, nor Quoy," continued Paganel, launched
like an express, "nor Bennett, nor Cunningham, nor
Mitchell, nor Tiers——"

"Have mercy!"

"Nor Dixon, nor Strelesky, nor Reid, nor Wilkes,
nor Mitchell——"

"Stop, Paganel," said Glenarvan, laughing heartily,
"do not overwhelm the poor fellow. Be generous!
He acknowledges himself beaten."

"And his rifle?" asked the geographer in triumph.

"It is yours, Paganel," answered the major, "and I
regret it much. But you have memory enough to gain
a whole museum of artillery. But, perhaps, all the
incidents relating to the discovery of Australia are not
so well known to you."

"If you can cite me one I don't know, I will give you
back your rifle, MacNabbs."

"Well, do you know why Australia does not belong
to France, or rather the reason the English give?"

"No, major," said Paganel, looking vexed.

"It is simply because Captain Baudin, who, however,
was not timid, in 1802 was so frightened by the croak-

ing of Australian frogs, that he weighed anchor as soon as possible, and fled, never to return."

"Why, the English call us 'frog-eaters!' People are not generally afraid of what they eat."

"That is what is said, at all events," said the major.

And that is how the famous Purdey, Moore, and Dickson rifle remained the property of Major Mac-Nabbs.

CHAPTER V.

CAPE BERNOUILLI.

HE Duncan only slightly deviated from her route during the remainder of her passage, which turned out very stormy. Captain Mangles weighed anchor on her west coast in longitude 136° 12″ and latitude 35° 07′, at Cape Catastrophe, situated at one of the points of South Australia, and 300 miles from Cape Bernoulli.

Between Cape Catastrophe and its companion, Cape Borda, formed by a promontory of Kangaroo Island, lies Investigator Strait, which leads to Spencer Gulf on the north and Saint Vincent Gulf on the south. On the eastern shore of the latter lies Port Adelaide, capital of the province of South Australia. This town, founded in 1836, contains 40,000 inhabitants, who are more occupied with cultivating its fertile soil, cultivating its grapes and oranges, and all its agricultural riches, than in great industrial enterprises. The Duncan had sustained some damage to her screw, which could

not be repaired at Adelaide, so that Glenarvan and the
captain took the following resolution: the Duncan
should sail round the Australian shore, seeking for
traces of the Britannia; it should stop at Cape Ber-
noulli to get information, and then go on to Melbourne,
where the damage could be repaired. Once the screw
repaired, the Duncan should go and cruise on the
eastern coast. The captain, therefore, profited by the
first fair wind to start, and two hours afterwards he
lost sight of Cape Catastrophe. The same evening
Cape Borda was doubled, and Kangaroo Island passed.
This is the largest of the smaller Australian islands,
and serves as a refuge for escaped convicts. Its aspect
was enchanting. Immense carpets of verdure covered
the stratified rocks of its shores. When it was discovered in 1802, innumerable bands of kangaroos were
bounding through its woods and across its plains. The
next day, while the Duncan was sailing alongside, her
boats were sent to visit the coast to obtain information.
She was then on the 36th parallel, and Glenarvan
wished to leave no point unexplored to the 38th.

During the day of the 18th of December, the yacht,
with all sail on, ran close along the shores of Encounter
Bay. It was there that, in 1828, the traveller Sturt
arrived, after discovering the Murray, the largest
river of South Australia. Unlike the verdant shores
of Kangaroo Island, its shores were uniformly low and
arid, with now and then a grey cliff or sand promontory, as barren as a polar continent.

During this navigation the boats were of great
service. The sailors did not complain. Glenarvan,
his inseparable companion Paganel, and young Robert,
almost always accompanied them. They wished to seek

for vestiges of the Britannia with their own eyes. The Australian shores were as mute on the subject as the Patagonian shores had been. However, till they attained the precise point indicated in the document, they felt hope.

It was thus that, on the 20th of December, they arrived at Cape Bernouilli, which terminates Lacepede Bay, without the smallest success. In fact, in two years there could not be left any remains of the Britannia, for the natives would take what the sea had spared. Then, Harry Grant and his two companions, made prisoners the moment the waves had thrown them on to the coast, had doubtless been carried into the interior of the continent.

But then one of Paganel's ingenious hypotheses fell to the ground. As long as the Argentine territory was in question, the geographer could affirm that the figures on the document related not to the scene of shipwreck but to the place of their captivity. The large Pampas rivers were there to carry the precious document to the sea. Here, on the contrary, in this part of Australia, there are very few water-courses that cross the 37th parallel; what is more, the Rio Colorado and the Rio Negro flow towards the sea across desert places, uninhabitable and uninhabited, whilst the principal Australian rivers, the Murray, Yarra, Torrens, and Darling either flow into one another, or flow into the ocean, through mouths which have become frequented roadsteads, ports where navigation is active. What probability was there, therefore, that a fragile bottle could come down these continually navigated rivers as far as the Indian Ocean?

Paganel recognised the difficulty in a discussion

raised on the subject by Major MacNabbs. It became evident that the degrees marked in the document only applied to the scene of shipwreck, and that consequently the bottle had been thrown into the sea at the spot. If, therefore, no traces of the Britannia could be met with at Cape Bernouilli, Lord Glenarvan would have nothing to do but to return to Europe. His search would have been fruitless, but he would have fulfilled his duty courageously and conscientiously. This thought made the passengers of the yacht sad, and Mary and Robert Grant despair. Whilst going to the shore with Lord and Lady Glenarvan, John Mangles, MacNabbs, and Paganel, the captain's two children knew that their father's fate was going to be decided irrevocably; for had not Paganel, in a preceding discussion, judiciously demonstrated that, if the ship had been wrecked on the eastern coast, the captain would have reached home long before?

"There is still hope," repeated Lady Glenarvan to the young girl seated next to her in the boat that was taking them to the land. "God's hand will not fail us!"

"Yes, Miss Grant," said the captain, "when men have exhausted all human resources, then Heaven interferes, and by some unforeseen event opens up fresh paths."

The boat touched land in a little natural creek between coral banks in a state of formation, which in time would form a belt of breakers on the south part of Australia. Such as they were, they could already destroy a ship, and the Britannia might have been wrecked upon them.

The passengers of the Duncan disembarked without

difficulty upon a perfectly desert coast. Cliffs, with stratified bands, formed a coast-line 60 to 80 feet high. It would have been difficult to scale these natural ramparts without either ladder or cramp-irons. Happily, half a mile further south, John Mangles discovered a breach produced by a partial falling down of the cliff. The sea, doubtless, beat down the friable rock during its great equinoctial fits of anger, and thus determined the fall of the upper portion.

Glenarvan and his companions reached the top after a rather steep ascent. Robert climbed like a cat and reached the top first, to the despair of Paganel, who was humiliated at seeing his long legs of forty vanquished by little legs of twelve. The travellers soon reunited and examined the plain which stretched before them. It was a vast uncultivated district, which Glenarvan compared to the glens of the Scotch Lowlands, and Paganel to the unfertile lands of Brittany. But, although this country appeared uninhabited along the coast, the presence of man revealed itself in the distance.

" A mill !" cried Robert.

In fact, the sails of a mill were turning in the wind three miles off.

"Yes, it is a mill," answered Paganel, who had just looked at the object in question through his field-glass.

"We will go to it," replied Glenarvan.

After half an hour's walk, the ground changed abruptly from barren to cultivated country. Hedges surrounded freshly inclosed fields ; a few oxen, and half a dozen horses, were pasturing in the meadows, surrounded by robust acacias taken from the vast woods of Kangaroo Island. Little by little appeared fields covered with cereals, some acres of ground bristling with yellow ears, haycocks raised up like vast beehives, orchards, fine gardens worthy of Horace, then outbuildings, and at last a simple and comfortable habitation, overlooked by the joyous mill, and caressed by the moving shadow of its large sails.

At that moment a man of about fifty, of a prepossessing countenance, came out of the principal house, as four large dogs barked at the strangers. Five strong and handsome boys, his sons, followed him with their mother, a tall and robust woman. Glenarvan saw at once that it was an emigrant Irishman and his family. He had not time to speak before the man said—

"Strangers, welcome to the house' of Paddy O'Moore."

"Are you Irish?" said Glenarvan, taking the hand offered him by the colonist.

"I was," answered Paddy, "but now I am Australian. Come in, gentlemen; whoever you are, you are at home."

There was nothing for it but to accept unceremoniously so graceful an invitation. Lady Glenarvan and Mary Grant, conducted by Mrs. O'Moore, entered the habitation, whilst the sons of the colonist relieved their visitors of their arms.

A vast room, cool and light, occupied the ground-floor of the house, constructed of stout horizontal joists. A few wooden forms, nailed to the gaily-painted walls, a dozen stools, two oak dressers, on which white china and tin things shone, a long and wide table, at which twenty people could comfortably seat themselves, formed the furniture worthy of the solid house and its robust inhabitants.

The mid-day meal was on the table. A soup-tureen was smoking between a gigantic piece of roast beef and a leg of mutton, surrounded by large plates of olives, grapes, and oranges. The host seemed so engaging, the table looked so tempting and so abundantly spread, that it would have been rude not to accept. The farm servants, their master's equals, had already come to partake of their repast. Paddy O'Moore pointed to the place reserved for strangers.

"I expected you," said he, simply, to Lord Glenarvan.

"You expected us!" he answered, much astonished.

"I always expect strangers," answered the Irishman.

Then in a grave voice, whilst his family and servants stood respectfully, he said grace. Lady Glenarvan felt quite touched at such perfect simplicity of customs, and a look from her husband assured her that he admired it as much as she did.

While they were eating, Paddy O'Moore told his history. It was that of all emigrants whom poverty drives from their native land. Many come to seek a fortune, and only meet with misfortune. They accuse fate instead of their want of intelligence, idleness, and vice. The sober and courageous, economical and brave, always succeed.

Such had been, and such was, Paddy O'Moore. He left Dundalk, where he was dying of hunger, and went to Australia; disembarked at Adelaide, and began his career of agriculturist, to which he owed his present prosperity. All the territory of South Australia is divided into portions of 30 acres. These different lots are ceded to the colonists by the Government, and by each lot a laborious agriculturist can earn enough to

live on and put aside a nett sum of £80. Paddy
O'Moore knew that. He lived, economised, acquired
fresh lots with the profits of the first. His family and
farm both prospered. The Irish peasant became a landed
proprietor, and, although his farm was only two years
old, he then possessed 500 acres of soil reclaimed by
his labour, and 500 heads of cattle. He was his own
master after having been a slave in Europe, and as
independent as he could be in the freest country in the
world.

When Paddy O'Moore's story was told, he doubtless
expected confidence for confidence, but did not ask for
it. He was one of those discreet people who say,
"That is what I am, but I do not ask you what you
are." Glenarvan had an immediate interest in speaking of the Duncan, of his presence at Cape Bernouilli,
and the search which he was pursuing with indefatig-
able persoverance, and like a man who goes straight to
his point, he questioned Paddy O'Moore about tho
shipwreck of the Britannia. The Irishman's answer
was not favourable. He had never heard about the
ship. For the last two years no ship had been lost on
that coast either above or below the Cape.

"Now, my lord," added he, "may I ask you what
interest you have in asking me that question?"

Then Glenarvan related the history of the document
to the colonist, the voyage of the yacht, and all they
had done to find Captain Grant; he did not hide that
his dearest hopes fell before such precise affirmations,
and that now he despaired of ever finding the shipwrecked mariners again. Such words could not but
produce a painful impression on Glenarvan's audience.
The eyes of Mary and Robert filled with tears as they

listened. Paganel did not find a word of consolation or hope. John Mangles suffered to see a grief which he could not assuage. Despair had taken possession of the generous men whom the Duncan had brought in vain to these far-off coasts when these words were heard.

" My lord, praise and bless God. If Captain Grant is alive, he is on Australian soil!"

CHAPTER VI.

AYRTON.

T would be impossible to depict the surprise that these words produced. Glenarvan jumped up and pushed back his chair.

" Who spoke?" said he.

" I did," answered one of the servants seated at the end of the table.

" You, Ayrton?" said O'Moore, not less astonished than Glenarvan.

" Yes," answered Ayrton, in a firm voice. " I, a Scotchman like you, my lord, and one of the ship-wrecked men from the Britannia."

This declaration produced an indescribable effect Mary Grant nearly fainted with emotion, whilst John Mangles, Robert, and Paganel left their places and went towards the individual whom Paddy O'Moore had called Ayrton.

He was a man of forty-five, of rude features, whose brilliant eyes were hidden under bushy eyebrows. He was thin, but looked strong. He was all bones and muscles, and had lost no time in making fat. Middle height, broad shoulders, decided manner, a face full of intelligence and energy, all prepossessed in his favour. The sympathy which he inspired was still increased by the traces of recent sorrow imprinted on his face. They saw that he had suffered, and suffered much, although he looked like a man who could bear suffering and conquer it. Glenarvan and his friends felt that at first sight. Glenarvan began to question him. The meeting of Glenarvan and Ayrton had evidently produced a reciprocal emotion in both of them.

" Were you wrecked in the Britannia ?" asked Lord Glenarvan.

" Yes, my lord; I was quartermaster under Captain Grant," answered Ayrton.

" Were you saved with him after the shipwreck ?"

" No, my lord, no. I was swept off the deck and carried to the shore."

" Then you are not one of the two sailors mentioned in the document ?"

" No; I did not know of the existence of this document. I thought that Captain Grant was drowned, and that I was the only survivor."

" But you said Captain Grant was alive."

" No; I said if Captain Grant is alive——"

" And you added, he is on the Australian continent."

" Yes, he cannot be anywhere else."

" Where did the shipwreck take place, then ?" said Major MacNabbs.

That ought to have been the first question; but in the confusion caused by this incident, Glenarvan, who was in a hurry to know where Captain Grant was, forgot to ask where the Britannia had been lost.

"When I was swept off the deck," answered Ayrton, "the Britannia was running on to the Australian coast. It was not two cables off. The shipwreck must have happened then."

"In what latitude?" asked Mangles.

"Thirty-seven degrees," answered Ayrton.

"On the west coast?"

"No, on the east," answered Ayrton, quickly.

"At what epoch?"

"In the night of June 27, 1862."

"The very same!" cried Glenarvan.

"You see, my lord," added Ayrton, "that I could rightly say if Captain Grant still lives, he must be sought for on the Australian continent, and nowhere else."

"And we will seek him, and find him, and save him!" cried Paganel. "Ah! precious document!" added he, with perfect naïveté, "you fell into good hands."

No one heard Paganel's flattering words. They were all shaking hands with Ayrton. It seemed as though the presence of this man was a certain warrant of Captain Grant's safety. Why could not the captain escape as well as this sailor? Ayrton replied to the thousand questions with which he was assailed with remarkable intelligence and precision. Whilst he was talking, Mary Grant held one of his hands in hers. This sailor had been one of her father's companions, had run the same dangers! Mary could not take her eyes off the rough face, and wept with happiness.

Until now, no one had thought of doubting the veracity and identity of the quartermaster. The major, and perhaps John Mangles, were the only two

D

who asked themselves if Ayrton deserved entire confidence. Ayrton had certainly quoted facts and dates which agreed in striking particulars. But, however exact, these details did not prove the fact, and it is generally remarked that a lie is affirmed by precision of details. MacNabbs, therefore, reserved his opinion, and refrained from pronouncing it.

As to John Mangles, his doubts soon melted before the sailor's words, especially when he heard him speak to Mary about her father. Ayrton knew Mary and Robert perfectly. He had seen them at Glasgow on the departure of the Britannia. He remembered their presence at the farewell dinner on board, at which the sheriff MacIntyre assisted. They had confided Robert, who was scarcely ten years old, to the care of Dick Turner, the boatswain, and he escaped and climbed to the gallant-sail.

" So I did! so I did!" said Robert.

And Ayrton recalled a thousand little incidents, without appearing to attach the same importance to them as John Mangles did. When he paused, Mary said to him in her gentle voice—

" Speak to me again about my father, Mr. Ayrton."

The quartermaster satisfied the desires of the young girl as well as he was able. Glenarvan would not interrupt him, though he thought of a thousand useful questions; but Lady Glenarvan showed him Mary's joyful emotion, and stopped him. It was in this conversation that Ayrton recalled the story of the Britannia and its voyage across the seas of the Pacific. Mary Grant knew a great part of it, as she had received news from her father up to the month of May, 1862. During that period of the year Captain Grant

touched at the Hebrides, New Guinea, New Zealand,
New California, meeting with difficulties from present
proprietors, many of whom were little justified in being
so, and the English authorities, for his ship was known
in the British colonies. However, he had found an important point on the western coast of Papua; it appeared easy to establish a Scotch colony there, and its
prosperity seemed assured; in fact, a good port to put
into on the route to the Moluccas and Philippines
must attract ships—above all, when the piercing of the
isthmus of Suez would supplant the Cape route. Captain Grant predicted M. de Lesseps' success, and was
not one of those who throw political rivalry across
great international interest.

After reconnoitring Papua, the Britannia went to
revictual at Callao, and she left this port on May 30th,
1862, to return to Europe by the Indian Ocean and
the Cape route. Three weeks afterwards a fearful
tempest assailed the ship. They were obliged to dis-
mast her, she sprang a leak, and the crew were worn
out with constant working at the pumps. For one week
the Britannia was the plaything of the storms. She
had six feet of water in her hold, and was gradually
sinking. The boats had been carried away by the
tempest. On the night of the 22nd of June they
sighted the Australian coast. The ship was thrown on
to the breakers with a violent shock, Ayrton was washed
off, and lost consciousness. When he came to himself,
he was in the hands of the natives, who dragged him
into the interior of the continent. From that time he
heard nothing more of the Britannia, and supposed, not
without reason, that she and all on board had perished
on the dangerous breakers of Twofold Bay. That was

all Ayrton knew about Captain Grant, but his own history after the shipwreck must be as interesting. In
fact, thanks to the document, it could not be doubted
that Grant and his two sailors had survived the shipwreck as Ayrton himself had done. Ayrton was, therefore, asked to relate his own adventures. His tale was
very short and very simple. He had been carried
away by a native tribe to the interior regions watered
by the Darling—that is to say, 400 miles north of the
37th parallel. There he lived very miserably, because
the tribe was a miserable one, but he was not ill-treated.
These were two long years of painful slavery. However,
he hoped to recover his liberty, and watched for the
least chance of escaping, although his flight must throw
him amidst innumerable dangers.

One night in October, 1864, he eluded the vigilance
of the natives, and disappeared in the depths of immense forests. For one month living on roots, edible
ferns, the gum of mimosas, he wandered amidst these
vast solitudes, guiding himself by the sun by day and
the stars by night. He crossed marshes, rivers, mountains, all that uninhabited portion of the continent
which rare travellers alone have crossed. At last, half
dead with exhaustion, he reached the hospitable habitation of Paddy O'Moore, where he found a happy
existence in exchange for his work.

" And I am glad mine was the first house he reached,"
said the colonist, " for he has proved an intelligent and
industrious workman, and my house shall remain his as
long as he pleases."

Ayrton thanked the Irishman with a gesture, and
waited for fresh questions, though he, doubtless, thought
there could not be many more to ask him. What could

he answer henceforth except what he had already said a hundred times? Glenarvan was going to open a discussion as to what must be done next, when the major said to him—

"You were quartermaster on board the Britannia?"

"Yes," answered Ayrton, unhesitatingly, but understanding that some slight doubt on the major's part must have dictated the question, he added, " I saved my engagement paper from the wreck, I will go and fetch it."

His absence did not last a minute, but Paddy O'Moore had time to say—

"My lord, Ayrton is an honest man. During the two months he has been in my service I have not had one complaint to make of him. He had told me all about his shipwreck and captivity before. I am sure he is a man worthy of all your confidence."

Glenarvan was going to reply that he had never doubted Ayrton's good faith, when the quartermaster entered with the paper. It was signed by the owners of the Britannia and Captain Grant; Mary Grant recognised her father's handwriting. All doubt about Ayrton's identity was now no longer possible.

"Now," said Glenarvan, "we must decide what is to be done next. Ayrton, your advice will be precious, and I shall be greatly obliged to you for it."

Ayrton reflected for some minutes, and then answered—

"I thank you, my lord, for the confidence you have in me, and I hope to show myself worthy of it. I have some knowledge of this country, and the customs of the natives, and if I can be of any use——"

"You certainly can," answered Glenarvan.

"I think, like you," answered Ayrton, "that Captain Grant and two sailors escaped from the wreck; but as they have not reached the English possessions, their fate must have been the same as mine, and they are prisoners of some native tribe."

"You repeat there some of my arguments," said Paganel. "They are evidently prisoners; but do you think that, like you, they have been carried to the north of the 37th parallel?"

"I expect so, sir; for the natives do not remain in the neighbourhood of the English districts."

"How will it be possible to find any traces of the prisoners in the interior of so vast a continent?" said Glenarvan.

This question was followed by a prolonged silence. Lady Glenarvan questioned each of her companions with a look, but obtained no answer. Even Paganel was silent. His ordinary ingenuity had forsaken him. John Mangles walked up and down the room as if he had been on the deck of his ship.

"And you, Mr. Ayrton," then said Lady Glenarvan, "what should you do?"

"My lady," answered Ayrton, quickly, "I should re-embark, and take the Duncan to the spot where the Britannia was wrecked. There I should take counsel of circumstances, and, perhaps, of indications that hazard might furnish."

"Very well," said Glenarvan; "but we must wait till the Duncan is repaired."

"Is she damaged, then?" asked Ayrton.

"Yes," answered John Mangles.

"Much?"

"No; but we have not the tools necessary on board

One of the paddle-wheels is strained, and can only be repaired at Melbourne."

"Can't you go under sail?" asked the quartermaster.

"Yes, but if the wind is at all contrary, we shall be a long time getting to Twofold Bay, and even then we shall have to return to Melbourne."

"Well, let her go to Melbourne," cried Paganel, "and we will go without her to Twofold Bay."

"How shall we do that?" said John Mangles.

"By crossing Australia like we crossed America, along the 37th parallel."

"But the Duncan?" said Ayrton, laying peculiar emphasis on the word.

"The Duncan will join us, or we shall join the Duncan, as the case may be. If we find Captain Grant, we shall go to Melbourne with him. If we do not find him before we reach the coast, the Duncan must come to us there. Who has any objections to this plan? Has the major?"

"No," said MacNabbs, "not if it is practicable."

"So practicable is it," answered Paganel, "that I propose that Lady Glenarvan and Miss Grant accompany us."

"Are you speaking seriously, Paganel?" asked Lord Glenarvan.

"Very seriously, my lord. It is a journey of 350 miles, not more. By going twelve miles a day we shall accomplish it in a month—that is to say, the time necessary to repair the Duncan. Ah! if it was a question of crossing the Australian continent under its lowest latitude, across its greatest width, by immense deserts, destitute of water, where the heat is torrid—in short, of doing what the boldest travellers have not yet undertaken, it would be a different thing. But this 37th parallel crosses the province of Victoria, as English a country as could be, with roads, railways, and people. You could do it in a carriage, or, what would be preferable, in a cart. It is a journey from London to Edinburgh—nothing more."

"But the wild animals?" said Glenarvan, who wished to raise all possible objections.

"There are no wild animals in Australia."

"But the savages?"

"There are no savages under this latitude, and, in any case, they are not cruel like the New Zealanders."

"But the convicts?"

"There are no convicts in the southern provinces of Australia, only in the eastern. Victoria has not only repulsed them, but has made a law to exclude the liberated felons of the other colonies from its territories. The Government of Victoria has this very year threatened to withdraw its subsidy from the Peninsula Company if its ships continue to take coal in the ports of Western Australia, where convicts are admitted. What! you do not know that—you, an Englishman?"

"I am not an Englishman," answered Glenarvan.

"What Mr. Paganel says is perfectly right, then," said Paddy O'Moore. "Not only the Province of Victoria, but Southern Australia, Queensland, and even Tasmania, have agreed to keep convicts off their territory. Since I have been in this farm I have not heard of a single convict."

"For my part I never saw one," said Ayrton.

"You see, my friends," continued Jacques Paganel, "there are few savages, no wild animals, no male-

factors. There are few European countries of which
so much could be said. Well, is it agreed?"

"What do you say, Helena?" asked Lord Glenarvan.

"What we all do, Edward," answered Lady Glenarvan, turning to her companions; "let us start at
once."

CHAPTER VII.

THE DEPARTURE.

GLENARVAN was not in the habit of
losing any time between the adoption of
an idea and its execution. Paganel's
proposition once resolved upon, he immediately gave orders that the preparations for the journey should be ready in the briefest
delay possible. The departure was fixed for the day
after the morrow, the 22nd of December.

What results would follow from this journey? It
merely increased the sum of favourable chances. None
of them much expected to find the captain on the line of
the 37th parallel, which they were rigorously going to
follow, but perhaps it crossed the track, and, in any
case, it led straight to the scene of the wreck. That
was the principal point.

More, if Ayrton consented to accompany the travellers, to guide them across the forests of Victoria,
and lead them to the eastern coast, that would give
them another chance of success. Glenarvan particularly wished to get his useful assistance, and asked his
host if he would mind him proposing it to Ayrton.

Paddy O'Moore consented, not without regretting the loss of so excellent a servant.

"Well, Ayrton, will you accompany us on our expedition?" asked Glenarvan.

Ayrton did not answer immediately; he even appeared to hesitate for some minutes, and then said—

"Yes, my lord, I will go with you; and if I do not lead you on the track of Captain Grant, I shall at least guide you to the spot where the Britannia was lost."

"Thank you, Ayrton," answered Glenarvan.

"May I ask you one question, my lord?"

"Certainly."

"Where shall you meet the Duncan again?"

"At Melbourne, if we do not have to cross Australia from one shore to the other; in the eastern coast if we do."

"And the captain?"

"The captain will await my instructions at Melbourne."

"Very well, my lord, you may count upon me."

Glenarvan gave Ayrton the commission to get together the means of transport for this journey across Australia, and having arranged that business, the passengers returned on board after settling where to meet Ayrton.

When John Mangles gave his support to the proposition, he supposed that this time he should accompany the expedition. He begged it as a favour from Glenarvan, aducing all sorts of arguments in his favour; his devotion to Lady Glenarvan and his lordship himself, the use he could be in organising the caravan, and his inutility as captain on board the Duncan—in short, a thousand excellent reasons except the best, of which Glenarvan did not need to be convinced.

"Have you absolute confidence in your second, John?" asked Glenarvan.

"Absolute," answered Mangles. "Tom Austin is a good sailor. He will take the Duncan to her destination, and will have her repaired and ready by the day you fix. Tom is a slave to duty and discipline. He will never take upon himself to modify or retard the execution of an order. Your lordship may depend upon him as much as upon me."

"Then you may come, John," answered Glenarvan, "for," added he, smiling, "of course you would like to be with us if we find Mary's father."

Mangles looked confused as he took Glenarvan's proffered hand.

The next day, John Mangles, accompanied by the ship's carpenter and sailors loaded with provisions, returned to Paddy O'Moore's dwelling, in order to organise the means of transport in concert with the Irishman. All the family awaited him, ready to work under his orders. Ayrton was there to give them the benefit of his experience. Paddy and he agreed in deciding that the ladies were to make the journey in an ox-cart, and the men were to go on horseback. Paddy was able to procure the animals and the vehicle.

The vehicle was twenty feet long, and covered with a tarpaulin; it ran upon four round wooden wheels; it had shafts twenty-five feet long, in which six pairs of oxen could be yoked. These animals drew with their head and neck, by the double combination of a yoke fastened on their head, and a collar fastened to the

yoke with an iron collar-pin. Great skill was required
to conduct this long, narrow, oscillating machine, and to
drive the team by means of a goad. But Ayrton had
served his apprenticeship at the farm, and Paddy
answered for his skill. To him was, therefore, assigned
the task of driving.

The vehicle had no springs, and was far from comfortable; but such as it was, it was necessary to take it.
As John Mangles could change nothing in its rude
construction, he caused the interior to be arranged as
comfortably as possible. They divided it into two
compartments by means of a screen. The back part
was destined to receive the provisions, luggage, and
Mr. Olbinett's portable stove. The front was set apart
solely for the ladies. Under the carpenter's hand, this
first compartment was transformed into a convenient
chamber, covered with a thick carpet, and furnished
with a toilette-table and two bedsteads, reserved for
Lady Helena and Mary Grant. Thick leather curtains
closed it when necessary, and defended it against the
night air. In case of great rain, the men could take
refuge in it, but a tent was to be their usual shelter in
the hours of encampment. John Mangles did his
utmost to unite in the narrow space all the objects
necessary to two women, and he succeeded. Lady
Glenarvan and Mary Grant were not destined to regret,
in their rolling room, the comfortable cabins of the
Duncan.

It was easier to provide for the men; seven vigorous
horses were procured for Lord Glenarvan, Paganel,
Robert Grant, MacNabbs, John Mangles, and the two
sailors, Wilson and Mulrady, who were to accompany
their master in this new expedition. Ayrton, of course

had his place on the driver's seat, and Mr. Olbinett, whom equitation tempted little, could put up with travelling in the luggage compartment. Horses and oxen were grazing in the farm meadows, and could easily be assembled when it was time to start. That settled, and his orders given to the ship's carpenter, John Mangles returned on board with the Irish family. Ayrton accompanied them, and about four p.m they were all on the deck of the Duncan.

They were received with open arms. Glenarvan offered them dinner on board, and his guests willingly accepted. Paddy was filled with admiring astonishment. The cabin furniture, the hangings, the maple and rosewood panneling, excited his admiration. Ayrton, on the contrary, only gave moderate approbation to these costly superfluities, while he examined the yacht from a sailor's point of view; he visited the hold and the engine-room ; asked about the power of the engine and its consummation; explored the coal stores, powder-room, and steward's room; and interested himself particularly in the arms and the forecastle cannon. Glenarvan had to do with a man who knew what he was about, he saw that by Ayrton's questions, especially when he was examining the masts and rigging.

"You have a handsome ship here, my lord," said he. "What is her tonnage ?"

"She gauges 210 tons."

"Shall I be far out if I guess her speed, with all steam on, at fifteen knots ?" added Ayrton.

"Add two," said Mangles, "and you will be right."

"Seventeen!" said the quartermaster, "then there is no ship of war—not even the best ever made—that could catch her."

"Not one!" answered Mangless. "The Duncan is a racing yacht, and could not be beaten anyhow."

"Not even under sail?" asked Ayrton.

"No, not even then."

"Well, my lord, and you, captain," answered Ayrton, "allow a sailor who knows a good ship when he sees her, to congratulate you."

"Well, Ayrton," answered Glenarvan, "it only depends upon yourself whether she becomes your ship or no."

"I will think about it, my lord," answered the quartermaster, simply.

Mr. Olbinett came up at that moment to inform his lordship that dinner was ready. Glenarvan and his guests went towards the saloon.

"An intelligent man that Ayrton," said Paganel to the major.

"Too intelligent!" answered MacNabbs, who, without the shadow of a reason, had taken a dislike to the quartermaster.

During dinner Ayrton gave many interesting details about the Australian continent, which he knew perfectly. He asked how many sailors Glenarvan meant to take with him in his expedition. When he learned that Mulrady and Wilson only were going he appeared astonished. He tried to persuade Glenarvan to form his troop of the best sailors of the Duncan, and insisted so much that it ought to have effaced all suspicion from the major's mind.

"But," said Glenarvan, "our journey across South America offers no danger?"

"None," answered Ayrton, quickly.

"Then it is better to leave as many sailors as pos-

sible on board for manœuvres and repairs. It is of
great consequence that she should be punctual at our
meeting place, so we had better not lessen the crew."

Ayrton seemed to understand Lord Glenarvan's
observation, and did not insist.

When evening came, the Scotch and Irish separated.
Ayrton and Paddy O'Moore returned to their habitation.
Horses and waggon were to be ready for the next day.
The departure was fixed for eight a.m.

Lady Glenarvan and Mary Grant then made their
last preparations. They were shorter and less minute
than those of Jacques Paganel. The savant passed
a part of the night in unscrewing, wiping, and putting his telescope together again. He was still asleep
when the major called him at daybreak.

John Mangles had already sent the luggage to the
farm. A boat was waiting for the travellers, who took
their places in it. The young captain gave his last
orders to Tom Austin, and recommended him especially
to await Lord Glenarvan's orders at Melbourne; whatever they might be, he was to carry them out scrupulously. The old sailor answered that Mangles might
depend upon him. In the name of the crew he presented to his lordship their best wishes for the success
of the expedition. As the boat rowed off, the crew
gave three cheers.

Ten minutes after the boat touched the shore. A
quarter of an hour later the travellers arrived at the
farm. Everything was ready, and Lady Glenarvan was
delighted with the arrangement of her compartment.
The immense waggon, with its primitive wheels, pleased
her particularly. Ayrton, goad in hand, was awaiting
the orders of his new master.

" This is an admirable vehicle !" said Paganel, " it is worth all the mail coaches in the world. I know no better means of going about the world than in a house on wheels."

" M. Paganel," answered Lady Glenarvan, " I hope to have the pleasure of receiving you in my *salon.*"

" I shall be delighted, madame. Which is your day ?"

" I shall be at home every day for my friends," answered Helena, laughing, " and you are——"

"The most devoted of all, madame," answered the Frenchman, gallantly.

This exchange of politeness was interrupted by the arrival of the seven horses all ready harnessed. Lord Glenarvan settled with the Irishman the price of his different acquisitions, adding many thanks, which the brave colonist esteemed as much as the money.

The signal for departure was given. Lady Glenarvan and Miss Grant took their places in their compartment, Ayrton on the driver's seat, Olbinett at the back of the waggon ; Glenarvan, the major, Paganel, Robert, John Mangles, the two sailors, all armed with rifles and revolvers, mounted their horses. A " God help you !" was said by Paddy O'Moore, and his family repeated it in chorus. Ayrton uttered a peculiar cry, and incited his team. The waggon moved, and soon disappeared in a turn of the road from the hospitable farm of the worthy Irishman.

CHAPTER VIII.
THE PROVINCE OF VICTORIA.

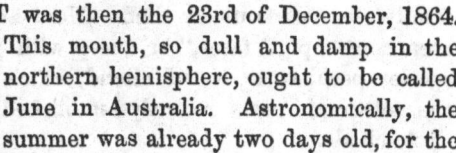T was then the 23rd of December, 1864. This month, so dull and damp in the northern hemisphere, ought to be called June in Australia. Astronomically, the summer was already two days old, for the sun had reached Capricorn on the 21st, and its presence above the horizon was already some moments shorter. It was, therefore, the warmest season of the year, and Lord Glenarvan's journey was to take place under the rays of an almost tropical sun.

The colonies of the great ocean island are actually six in number; New South Wales, capital Sydney; Victoria, capital Melbourne; South Australia, capital Adelaide; Queensland, capital Brisbane; West Australia, capital Perth; and North Australia, still without a capital. The coasts only are peopled by colonists. There is hardly one important town 200 miles inland. The interior of the continent—that is to say, an extent of country equal to two-thirds of Europe—is nearly unknown.

Happily the 37th parallel does not cross these immense solitudes, which have already cost so many victims to science. Glenarvan had only to do with the south of Australia, comprising a narrow portion of Adelaide, the whole width of Victoria, and the summit of the triangle, turned upside down, which forms New South Wales.

No order of march was scrupulously followed, each traveller could do as he liked within certain limits, they could sweep the plain and hunt, or stay and talk to the inhabitants of the waggon. Paganel did both.

E

The crossing of Adelaide was not interesting; it consisted of what is called bush, which in parts furnishes a scanty saline herbage, of which the ovine family seem particularly fond. Here and there were seen some "pigs' faces," or sheep with pigs' heads, a species peculiar to New Holland, which feed amongst the telegraph posts recently established on the coast of Adelaide.

About three p.m. the waggon crossed a large space destitute of trees, known under the name of "Mosquito Plains." The savant had the geographer's satisfaction of knowing that it deserved its name. The travellers and their horses suffered intensely from the bites of these importunate diptera; it was impossible to avoid them, and ammoniac was in great request. Paganel's long body was bitten from head to foot, and he required all his philosophy to support the pain.

Towards evening some hedges of acacias made gay the plain; here and there stood white gum trees; farther on was a freshly-beaten track, then trees of European origin, olives, lemon trees, and green oaks, and, lastly, good palisading. At eight o'clock the oxen, hurried on by Ayrton's goad, reached Red Gum station.

The word "station" is applied to the interior establishments where cattle are reared. The cattle farmers there are called squatters. Red Gum station is unimportant, but Glenarvan found the frankest hospitality there. The table is invariably laid for strangers under the roof of these solitary habitations, and an Australian colonist is always an obliging host.

The next day Ayrton harnessed his team at daybreak. He wished to reach the frontier of Victoria that evening. The ground became more and more un-dulated. A succession of little hills, all powdered with scarlet sand, appeared. The plain was like an immense red flag, under which the wind had got and made pleats. A few "malleys," a sort of pine spotted white, with a straight smooth trunk, spread their branches and dark green foliage over fat meadows filled with cattle. Later on they came to vast tracts of bush and young gum-trees, and lastly, isolated shrubs appeared, and presented the first specimens of native Australian trees.

As they approached the frontier of Victoria, the aspect of the country was sensibly modified. The travellers felt that they were at last in a new country.

After a journey of sixty miles, accomplished in two days, the caravan reached the parish of Aspley, the first town in Victoria, situated on the 141st degree of longitude, in the district of Wimerra.

The waggon was put up at the Crown Inn, and supper, composed solely of sheep, cooked in every way, was soon smoking on the table.

They ate much, but talked more. They all wanted to know more about the Australian continent, and asked the geographer numerous questions about it. Paganel told them all about Victoria, which was named Australia Felix.

"False qualification!" said he. "They would have done better to call it Rich Australia, for countries are like people, riches do not make their happiness. Aus-tralia, thanks to its coal mines, has been given up to needy adventurers. You will see that when we cross the gold district."

"Is not Victoria a colony of recent origin?" asked Lady Glenarvan.

"Yes, it has only been founded thirty years. It was on the 6th of June, 1835, a Tuesday."

"At 7.15 p.m.," answered the major, who liked to tease Paganel about the precision of his dates.

"No, at 7.10 p.m.," answered the geographer, seriously, "that Batman and Falckner founded a settlement at Port Phillip, on the bay where now stands the large town of Melbourne. For fifteen years the colony formed part of New South Wales. But, in 1851, it was declared independent, and took the name of Victoria."

"Has it prospered well since?" asked Glenarvan.

"Judge by the figures given in the last statistics; and whatever MacNabbs may say, I know nothing more eloquent than figures."

"Go on," said the major.

"I am going on. In 1836, the colony of Port Phillip had 244 inhabitants. To-day, the Province of Victoria contains 550,000. Seven millions of vine plants give annually 121,000 gallons of wine. A hundred and three thousand horses gallop across its plains, and 675,272 horned animals graze on its immense pasturages."

"Did you give the number of pigs?" asked MacNabbs.

"No, but I will. There are 79,625."

"And how many sheep, Paganel?"

"There are 7,115,943, MacNabbs."

"Including the one we are now eating, Paganel?"

"No, without it, for it is three parts eaten."

"Bravo, M. Paganel!" cried Lady Glenarvan, laughing heartily. "MacNabbs will not find you at fault."

"It is my trade to know those things. You may believe me when I tell you that this strange country is full of marvels."

"Up till now, however——" said the major.

"But wait a little, impatient major," cried Paganel. "You have scarcely set foot on the frontier, and you are complaining already. Well, I say, and repeat, and sustain, that this is the most curious country in the world. Its formation, nature, products, climate, and even its future disappearance, have astonished, do astonish, and will astonish, all the savants of the world. In this country the edges rose above the waves before the centre, like a gigantic ring, and perhaps there still exists a half-evaporated inland sea in the interior; its rivers dry up from day to day; there is no humidity, either in the air or ground; its trees annually lose their bark instead of their leaves; these leaves turn sideways, and not fully to the sun, and give no shadow; wood is often incombustible; stones melt away in the rain; forests are low, and grass gigantic; quadrupeds have beaks; the kangaroo has unequal legs; sheep have pigs' heads; foxes fly from tree to tree; swans are black; rats make nests; the "bower-bird" opens its drawing-rooms for the reception of its winged friends; birds astonish the imagination by the diversity of their songs and aptitudes. One serves as a clock, another makes a sound like a postilion's whip, another imitates the knifegrinder, another beats the seconds like the pendulum of a clock, one laughs when it gets up in the morning, and another weeps as it goes to bed at night. Oh, strange and illogical country! Well did Grimard say you were a sort of parody of universal laws, a defiance thrown in the face of the rest of the world!"

Certainly, after this enumeration of Australian singu-
arities, no one would think of asking Paganel for more.
But the major's reasoning instincts were too strong, and
he said—

"Is that all, Paganel?"

"Well, no, it is not all!" answered the savant, with
vehemence.

"Is there anything else astonishing in Australia?"
asked Lady Glenarvan, much astonished.

"Yes, there is its climate, stranger still than its productions. I do not speak of its healthiness, due to its
being so rich in oxygen and so poor in azote; it has no
damp winds, for the trade winds blow parallel with its
coasts, and most maladies are unknown in it, from
typhus to measles and chronic affections."

"However, that is not a slight advantage," said
Glenarvan.

"Certainly, but I do not speak of that," answered
Paganel. "Here the climate has a most astonishing
influence."

"What?" asked Mangles.

"You will never believe me."

"Yes, we shall."

"It has a moralising influence. Here metals do not
oxydise in the air, nor man either. Here the atmosphere dries and whitens everything rapidly—linen and
souls! They had taken the virtues of the climate into
account when they resolved to send people here to be
made moral."

"What, this influence is really felt?" asked Lady
Glenarvan.

"Yes, on men and animals."

"Are you not joking, Mr. Paganel?"

"Certainly not. Horses and cattle are remarkably docile here. You will see."

"It is not possible !"

"But it exists. And malefactors, transported into this reviving and salubrious air, are regenerated in a few years. This effect is known to philanthropists. In Australia all characters improve."

"But then, Mr. Paganel, you, who are already so good," said Helena, "what will you become in this privileged land."

"Simply excellent," answered Paganel, "*tout simplement excellent.*"

CHAPTER IX.

WIMERRA RIVER.

HEY started at daybreak the next day— December 24th. The heat was very great, but endurable, the route almost level, and easy for the horses. In the evening, after a good day's march, 'they encamped on the shores of Lake Blanche, and saw its brackish waters.

There Jacques Paganel was forced to agree that this lake was not white, any more than the Black Sea is black, or the Red Sea red, the Yellow River yellow, or the Blue Mountains blue. Mr. Olbinett prepared the evening meal with his habitual punctuality, and the travellers went to sleep in the waggon and under the tent, notwithstanding the lamentable howlings of the "dingos," the Australian jackals.

An admirable plain, covered with chrysanthemums,

extended beyond Lake Blanche. Meadows and flowers, in all their spring beauty, stretched to the limits of the horizon. The blue of the small-leaved flax mixed with the scarlet of an acanthus peculiar to the country. Numerous varieties of eremophilas lightened up this verdure, and the ground, impregnated with salt, disappeared under the anserines, arroches, beets, some glaucous, others red, all the family of the salsolaceans, which give excellent soda by the incineration and washing of their cinders. Paganel, who became a botanist amongst flowers, called all these varied productions by their names, and he told them that there were 4,200 species of plants, divided into 120 families in the flora of Australia.

Later on, after ten miles of road, the waggon wound amongst high thickets of acacias, mimosas, and white gum-trees with such variable inflorescence. The vegetable kingdom, in this country of the " Spring Plains," rendered up in perfumes and colours what the sun gave it in rays.

As to the animal kingdom, it was more avaricious in its productions. A few cassowaries bounded across the plain without it being possible to approach them. However, the major skilfully planted a bullet in the side of a very rare animal that has a tendency to disappear. It was a "jabiru," the giant crane of English colorists. It was five feet high, and its black beak, wide and conical, with pointed end, measured eighteen inches long. The violet and purple shades on its head, the lustrous green of its neck, the sparkling white of its throat, and bright red of its long legs, made it seem as if Nature had exhausted her palette of primitive colours in its formation.

This bird was much admired, and the major would have carried off the honours of the day if Robert had not killed a shapeless animal, half hedgehog, half antbear, a half-formed animal like those of the first ages of creation. A tongue, long and sticky, hung out of its toothless jaws and fished up the ants, which formed its principal food.

"It is an echidna!" said Paganel, giving its veritable name to this monothreme. "Have you ever seen such an animal?"

"It is horrible," answered Glenarvan.

"Horrible, but curious," replied Paganel, "and what is more, peculiar to Australia."

Of course Paganel wanted to take away the hideous echidna and put it in the luggage compartment, but Mr. Olbinett objected with such indignation that the savant gave up the pleasure of keeping his specimen.

Up till now the travellers had met with few colonists or squatters. The country seemed uninhabited. Of natives there was not the shadow, for the savage tribes wander more northwards across the immense solitudes watered by the Darling and the Murray. But a curious spectacle awaited the travellers; it was given to them to see one of those immense droves of cattle which enterprising speculators brought from the eastern mountains to Victoria and South Australia.

Towards four p.m. a column of dust appeared on the horizon. No one could make it out till Ayrton told them it was caused by cattle marching. As it approached, a concert of bleating, neighing, and bellowing, mixed with the human voice, whistling, shouting, or vociferating, was heard.

A man emerged from the moving cloud. He was

the chief conductor of this four-legged army. Glenarvan went up to him and began a conversation. He
was a "stock-keeper," and proprietor of a part of the
drove, which consisted of 12,075 head of cattle, 1,000
oxen, 11,000 sheep, and 75 horses. All these animals
were bought lean in the Blue Mountains, and were
going to be fattened in the pasturages of South Australia,
where they are sold again with a large profit.

Sam Mitchell, as the stock-keeper was called, gained
£2 on an oxen and 10s. on a sheep, and would realise
a sum of £6,000. It was much; but what patience and
energy are required to lead such an immense drove!
The gain is hardly earned.

Sam Mitchell told his story briefly, while the cattle
continued their march amongst the thickets of mimosas.
Lady Glenarvan, Mary Grant, and the horsemen, had
dismounted, and, seated in the shade of a vast gum-tree,
they listened to the stock-keeper's story.

Sam Mitchell had started seven months before,
making about ten miles a day, and his journey would
last another ten days. He had with him, to help him
in his laborious task, twenty dogs and thirty men, five
of whom were blacks, skilful in tracking out wandering
animals. Six waggons followed the army. The drovers,
armed with stock-whips, with handles eighteen inches
and thongs nine feet long, circulated amongst the ranks,
establishing order, whilst the dogs' light cavalry kept
the flanks.

The travellers admired the discipline established in
the drove. The different races marched separately, for
wild oxen and sheep do not agree very well together;
the former will never graze where the latter have passed.
The oxen were, therefore, placed first, divided into two

battalions. Five regiments of sheep followed, driven by twenty drovers, and the horses brought up the rear.

Sam Mitchell made his auditors remark that the guides of his army were neither dogs nor men, but oxen, intelligent leaders whose superiority was recognised by their followers. They advanced in the front rank with perfect gravity, choosing a good road by instinct, and convinced of their right to be treated with respect. If they chose to stop, it was necessary to allow them to do so, and it was useless to attempt to set out again after a halt till they themselves gave the signal for departure.

Some details added by the stock-keeper completed the history of this expedition, worthy of being written, if not commanded, by Xenophon himself. Whilst the army was marching across a plain, all was well. There was little embarrassment or fatigue. The animals grazed along the route, drinking at the numerous creeks, sleeping at night, travelling by day, and reassembling with docility at the voice of the dogs. But in the large forests of the continent, across thickets of eucalyptus and mimosas, difficulties increased. The animals got mixed up together, or strayed away, and it took much time to get them in order of march again. If it happened that a leader was missing, it must be found again, or there would be a general helter-skelter, and the blacks often passed several days in the search. If the great rains were falling, the idle animals refused to advance, and in violent storms a panic took possession of the animals, and made them mad with terror.

However, by force of energy and activity, the stock-keeper triumphed over these difficulties. His patience was put to the most severe test when it was necessary

to cross a river, and the animals refused to cross it.
The oxen, after having swallowed a little water, retraced
their steps.   The sheep fled in every direction, rather
than face the liquid element.   They waited for night
to get the drove to the river, and that did not succeed.
They threw in the rams, and the ewes refused to follow
them.   They deprived them of water for several days,
but the drove did without drinking.   They carried the
lambs on to the other bank, hoping that the mothers
would come at their cries, the lambs bleated, but the
mothers stopped where they were.   That sometimes
lasted for a month, and the stock-keeper no longer knew
what to do with his bleating, neighing, and bellowing
army, when, one fine day, by caprice, no one knows
why or how, a detachment crosses the river, and then
there is another difficulty to prevent them throwing
themselves in headlong.   Confusion prevails in the
ranks, and many animals are drowned by the current.

Such were the details given by Sam Mitchell.   During
his tale, a great part of the drove had gone by in good
order.   It was time he rejoined the head of the army,
and chose the best pasturages.   He, therefore, took
leave of Glenarvan, sprang upon an excellent native
horse which one of his men was holding, and a few
minutes afterwards he had disappeared in the cloud of
dust.

The waggon went on in an opposite direction, and did
not stop again till it reached Mount Talbot in the
evening.   Paganel reminded his friends that it was
Christmas Day, but the steward had not forgotten it,
and a savoury supper, served under the tent, gained
him the sincere compliments of all.   Mr. Olbinett
had surpassed himself.   His reserve had furnished a

contingent of European food rarely met with in the deserts of Australia. A reindeer ham, slices of salted beef, smoked salmon, and oatmeal cake, plenty of tea, abundance of whiskey, and some bottles of port, composed this astonishing meal. Paganel added to it the fruit of a wild orange which grew at the foot of the hills. It was the "moccaly" of the natives; its oranges were a rather insipid fruit, but its crushed pippins were as hot as Cayenne pepper. The geographer was determined to eat them out of love to science, and set his palate on fire, so that he could not answer the questions with which the major overwhelmed him on the peculiarities of the Australian deserts.

The next day, December 26th, offered no incident of moment. They passed the springs of Norton Creek, and later on Mackenzie River, half dried up. The weather kept fine, but the heat was endurable; the wind blew from the south and cooled the atmosphere, as a north wind would do in the boreal hemisphere, which fact made Paganel say to Robert that it was a fortunate circumstance, for the heat is, on an average, greater in the southern than in the northern hemisphere.

"How is that?" asked the young boy.

"Have you never heard that the earth is nearer to the sun in the winter than it is in the summer?"

"Yes, Mr. Paganel."

"And that the cold of winter is due to the obliquity of the sun's rays?"

"Yes, I know that, too."

"Well, my boy, it is for that same reason that it is warmer in the southern hemisphere."

"I do not understand how," answered Robert.

"Reflect, then," continued Paganel. "When it is winter in Europe, what season is it here in Australia, our antipodes?"

"It is summer," answered Robert.

"Well, then, when it is summer in Australia, the earth is nearer the sun. Now do you understand?"

"Yes, Mr. Paganel. I never thought of that before."

"Then do not forget it again, my boy."

Robert ended his lesson in cosmography by learning that the average temperature of Victoria is 74°.

In the evening the caravan encamped five miles beyond Lake Lonsdale, between Mount Drummond on the north and the low summit of Mount Dryden on the south. The next day, at eleven a.m., the waggon reached the banks of the Wimerra, on the 143rd meridian.

The river, half a mile wide, flows through rows of gum-trees and acacias. A few magnificent myrtles, amongst others the "metrosideros speciosa," rose to a height of fifteen feet, with their long drooping branches and red flowers. Birds of brilliant colours fluttered in the green twigs. Below, on the surface of the water, floated a couple of wild black swans. This "rara avis" of Australian rivers was soon lost in the meanderings of the Wimerra.

In the meantime the waggon had stopped on a carpet of soft grass, extending to the rapid waters. There was neither bridge nor raft to carry them over. Ayrton looked for a practicable ford. The river appeared less deep a quarter of a mile up stream, and he chose that place. Different soundings only gave three feet of water, and the waggon could go through that without risk.

" Is there no other means of crossing the river?"
asked Glenarvan of the quartermaster.

" None, my lord," answered Ayrton; "but this passage does not seem dangerous; we can ford the river
here."

"Ought Lady Glenarvan and Miss Grant to leave
the waggon?"

" There is no need. My oxen are surefooted, and I
will take care to keep them straight."

" Very well, Ayrton," answered Glenarvan; "I trust
to you."

The horsemen surrounded the heavy vehicle, and
they entered the river. When waggons attempt to
ford they are generally surrounded by a chaplet of
empty casks, which keep them on the surface of the
water. But here this swimming belt was wanting, and
they were obliged to depend on the sagacity of the
oxen, held in hand by the prudent Ayrton, who, from
his seat, guided the team. The major and the two
sailors went on a few yards ahead. Glenarvan and
Mangles, on either side of the waggon, held themselves
ready to go to the help of the ladies. Paganel and
Robert brought up the rear.

All went well till they reached the middle of the
stream and the water came above the wheels. The
oxen there lost their footing and dragged the oscillating machine with them. Ayrton behaved very
courageously; he sprang into the water, and, holding
on to the horns of the oxen, he succeeded in putting
them in the right road. At that moment they came to
an unforeseen rise in the ground, and the waggon bent
under the shock; the water touched the ladies' feet,
and waggon and team began to drift, in spite of all

Glenarvan and John Mangles' efforts. It was a moment full of anxiety.

Happily, a vigorous pull drew the vehicle nearer the opposite bank, which sloped down to the water, so that the oxen and horses climbed it easily, and soon men and animals found themselves safe, not less satisfied than wet through. The fore part of the waggon had been broken by the shock, and Glenarvan's horse had lost its fore shoes. This accident demanded prompt reparation, and Ayrton proposed to go to Black Point Station, situated twenty miles to the north, and bring back a farrier.

"Go, Ayrton," said Glenarvan. "How much time shall you want to go and come back?"

"Fifteen hours, perhaps," answered Ayrton, "but not more."

"Go, then, and we will encamp here till you come back."

————

CHAPTER X.

THE RAILWAY FROM MELBOURNE TO SANDHURST.

HE major had not seen Ayrton leave the Wimerra encampment to seek a farrier at Black Point Station without apprehension. But he did not say a word about his private doubts, and contented himself with surveying the neighbourhood of the river. The tranquillity of these peaceful plains was troubled by nothing, and, after a few hours of darkness, the sun reappeared above the horizon.

Glenarvan's only fear was that Ayrton should come

back alone. If he did not find a workman the waggon could not set out again. The journey would be delayed for several days, and Glenarvan was impatient to reach his goal.

Happily, Ayrton lost no time, and he reappeared at daybreak the next day. A man accompanied him, who said he was a farrier from Black Point Station. He was a tall, muscular man, with a very low type of physiognomy, not at all prepossessing. It did not much matter, so that he knew his trade; anyway, he spoke very little, and uttered no useless words.

"Does he know his business?" asked John Mangles of the quartermaster.

"I do not know any more about him than you, captain," answered Ayrton. "We shall see."

The farrier set to work. He knew what he was about; that was shown by the way he mended the waggon. He worked skilfully, with no common strength. The major noticed that his wrists were marked with a ring of blackish flesh, and seemed to have been recently hurt; he asked the farrier about them, but the man did not answer, and went on with his work. Two hours afterwards the damage of the waggon was repaired, and the farrier soon shod Glenarvan's horse, for which he had brought the shoes all prepared. The major noticed that there was a trefoil roughly cut out of the back of these horseshoes, and pointed it out to Ayrton.

"It is the mark of Black Point," answered the quartermaster. "It allows them to follow the track of horses that stray from the station."

When the farrier had finished his work, he went away without having spoken four words. Half an hour

F

afterwards the travellers were again on their way. Beyond the curtain of mimosas extended an open plain. Some fragments of quartz and ferruginous rocks lay amongst the bushes, the tall herbs and palisades surrounding inclosures for animals. A few miles further on the wheels of the waggon sank into marshy ground, where murmured irregular creeks half hidden under a network of gigantic reeds. Then they passed vast salt lagoons in full evaporation. The journey went on pleasantly, and without fatigue.

Lady Glenarvan invited the horsemen to pay her a visit in turn, for her drawing-room was very small. They thus rested from the fatigue of riding, and enjoyed the conversation of that amiable woman. Lady Glenarvan, seconded by Miss Mary, did the honours of her house on wheels with perfect grace. John Mangles was not forgotten in these daily invitations, and his serious conversation did not displease; on the contrary.

It was thus that they crossed diagonally the mail road from Crowland to Horsham, a dusty highway little used by foot-passengers. A few low hills were passed at the extremity of the county of Talbot, and in the evening they reached a place three miles above Maryborough. A fine rain was falling, which in any other country would have made the ground wet, but here the air absorbed the humidity so marvellously that they could encamp as usual. The next day, the 29th of December, their journey was rather delayed by a series of low hills, which formed a miniature Switzerland. The ladies walked part of the way to avoid the continual jolting, and liked the change. At eleven o'clock they arrived at Carlsbrook, a rather important municipality. Ayrton did not advise them to go through the town—in order to gain time, he said. Glenarvan was of the same opinion; but Paganel, with laudable curiosity, wished to visit Carlsbrook. They let him do as he liked, and the waggon slowly continued its route.

Paganel, as usual, took Robert with him. He only stayed a short time, but it was enough to give him a pretty good idea of Australian towns. There was a bank, a town-hall, a market, a school, a church, and a hundred perfectly uniform brick houses, all built in a regular quadrilateral, crossed by parallel streets in the English fashion. Great activity reigned in the streets of Carlsbrook, a remarkable symptom in so young a town. It seems as if, in Australia, the towns grew like trees by the heat of the sun. Business men hurry along the streets, gold is carried along, escorted by the native police, to be sent away, coming from Bendigo or Mount Alexander. Every one, spurred on by interest, thought only of his own business, and the strangers passed unperceived in the midst of the laborious population.

After an hour employed in sightseeing, the two visitors rejoined their companions across carefully cultivated country. Long meadows, known under the name of " Low Level Plains," succeeded it, with innumerable flocks of sheep and shepherds' huts. Then the desert appeared without transition with the abruptness peculiar to Australian scenery. Simpson Hills and Mount Tarrangower mark the southern point of the district of Loddo on the 144th degree of longitude.

Up till now they had met with none of the native tribes living in a savage state. Paganel told Glenarvan that, under that latitude, the savages principally frequented the plains of the Murray, situated 100 miles to the east.

"We are approaching the gold country," said he. "In two days' time we shall be crossing the opulent region of Mount Alexander. It was there that miners flocked in 1852. The natives were obliged to fly to the interior deserts. We are in a civilised country, though it does not look like it, and our route, before the end of the day will cross the railway which puts the Murray in communication with the sea. A railway in Australia seems to me a very surprising thing!"

"Why, Paganel?" asked Glenarvan.

"Oh, because they don't harmonise! Oh, I know very well that you Englishmen, accustomed to colonise—you who have electric telegraphs and universal exhibitions in New Zealand—you find it quite natural. But in a Frenchman like me, it confuses all his ideas about Australia."

"Because you look at the past instead of the present," said Mangles.

"Agreed," answered Paganel; "but locomotives and mimosas, steam and eucalyptus, do not seem natural companions. I can't think of savages catching the 3.30 express to go from Melbourne to Kyneton, Castlemaine, Sandhurst, or Echuca, and no one could but an Englishman or an American. The poetry of the desert vanishes before your railways."

"What does it matter if progress follows in this path?" answered the major.

A very loud whistle interrupted the discussion. The travellers were not a mile from the railway. An engine, coming from the south with small speed, stopped precisely at the point of intersection between the railway and the road followed by the waggon.

This railway, as Paganel had said, joined the capital of Victoria to the Murray, the largest river in Australia. This immense stream, discovered by Sturt in 1828, comes from the Australian Alps, is increased by the Lachlan, and the Darling covers all the northern frontier of Victoria, and flows into Encounter Bay near Adelaide. It crosses rich and fertile countries, and the squatters' stations get more frequent along its line, thanks to the easy communications that the railway establishes with Melbourne. This railway was used for a length of 500 miles between Melbourne and Sandhurst, stopping at Kyneton and Castlemaine. The line in construction went on for seventy miles as far as Echuca, capital of the Riverine colony, founded that very year on the Murray.

The 37th parallel crosses this line of rails a few miles above Castlemaine, and precisely at Camden Bridge, over the Lutton, one of the numerous tributaries of the Murray. It was towards this point that Ayrton was driving his waggon, preceded by the horsemen, who galloped on to the bridge, attracted by a lively sentiment of curiosity. A considerable crowd was also going towards the railway. The inhabitants of the neighbouring stations left their houses, the shepherds their flocks. These words were repeatedly uttered—

"To the railway! to the railway!"

Some grave event must have happened to produce all that agitation. A great catastrophe, perhaps. Glenarvan, followed by his companions, hastened on. In a few minutes he reached Camden Bridge. There he soon saw what was the matter. A frightful accident

had taken place, not a meeting of trains, but a train
had run off the line and fallen into the river.

The river, which was crossed by the railway, was
encumbered by fragments of engines and carriages.
Five carriages out of six had been thrown into the bed
of the Lutton after the engine. The last carriage alone,
miraculously preserved by the rupture of the chain,
remained on the line a few yards from the abyss.

Glenarvan, Paganel, the major, and Mangles, mixed
with the crowd, and listened to what was said. Every
one was trying to explain the accident whilst they
worked at the ruins.

"The bridge broke down," said one.

"Why, it is still intact," said another. "They have
forgotten to close it for the passage of the train. That
is all!"

It was, in fact, a drawbridge made to allow boats to
pass. Had the guard, by unpardonable carelessness, forgotten to close it, and caused the train to rush with all
its express speed into the river? The accident had
happened in the night to the express No. 37, which had
started from Melbourne at 11.45 p.m. It must have
been 3.15 a.m. when the train, twenty-five minutes
after leaving Castlemaine Station, arrived at Camden
Bridge, and so met with its fate. The passengers and
the railway officials from the last carriage set about
getting help, but the telegraph posts lay on the ground,
and no message could be sent. It took three hours
before the authorities of Castlemaine could arrive on
the scene of disaster. It was six a.m. when a squadron
of police, under the direction of an inspector and Mr.
Mitchell, surveyor-general of the colony, arrived, and
help was obtained. The squatters and their men were

already doing all they could to put out the fire that had broken out amidst the ruins. There was no hope of withdrawing any living being from the furnace. Fire had rapidly finished the work of destruction. Ten only of the passengers survived, those who happened to be in the last waggon. The railway admiristration had sent an engine to take them back to Castlemaine.

In the meantime, Lord Glenarvan had made himself known to the surveyor-general, and talked with him and the inspector of police. This latter was a tall, thin man, imperturbably calm, who, if he had any sensibility in his heart, showed none in his face. He was contemplating the disaster like a mathematician would a problem, trying to solve it. Glenarvan said—

"What a fearful accident !"

"Worse than that, my lord."

"Worse than that !" cried Glenarvan, shocked at the phrase. "What could be worse ?"

"A crime !" answered the officer, calmly.

Glenarvan turned towards Mr. Mitchell and questioned him with a look.

"Yes, my lord," answered the surveyor-general, "our inquiry has led us to the certainty that the catastrophe is the result of a crime. The last carriage contained the luggage-van, and it has been pillaged. The surviving passengers were attacked by a band of five or six malefactors. The bridge was left open on purpose, not through carelessness ; and that fact, added to the disappearance of the guard, makes us conclude that he was an accomplice in the deed."

At this deduction of his superior, the police officer shook his head.

"You do not agree with my opinion?" asked Mr. Mitchell.

"No, I do not think the guard is an accomplice."

"But if the guard is not an accomplice, the crime could not have been committed by savages, for the mechanism of the drawbridge would be entirely unknown to them."

"True," answered the inspector.

"A boatman, who took his boat through Camden Bridge at 10.40 last night, says that the bridge was properly closed after his passage, so the guard must have assisted in the deed."

The inspector still shook his head.

"Then you do not attribute this crime to savages?"

"No, I do not."

"To whom, then?"

At that moment a murmur of voices was heard half a mile up the stream. It was caused by a crowd of men marching towards the station. As they drew near, Glenarvan saw two men amongst them carrying a corpse. It was the body of the guard, already cold. A dagger thrust in the heart had caused his death. The assassins, by dragging his corpse to some distance from Camden Bridge, wished to avert the suspicions of the police during their first inquiries. This discovery justified the doubts of the officer. Savages had had nothing to do with the crime.

"Those who did the deed," said he, "are men familiar with the use of this little instrument."

Speaking thus he exhibited a pair of "darbies," a species of handcuffs made of a double iron ring and furnished with a lock.

"Before long," he added, "I shall have the pleasure of offering them this bracelet as a Christmas gift."

"Then you suspect——"

"Men who have travelled gratis on board her Majesty's ships."

"What! convicts?" cried Paganel.

"I thought that convicts were not allowed on the soil of Victoria?" said Glenarvan.

"They are not allowed, but they come all the same," said the inspector. "I believe these came direct from Perth. Well, I'll take care they return there."

At that moment the waggon came in sight. Glenarvan wished to spare the ladies the horrible spectacle of Camden Bridge. He took leave of the surveyor-general, and signed to his friends to follow him.

"It is not a reason," said he, "for interrupting our journey."

Arrived at the waggon, Glenarvan spoke simply to his wife of a railway accident, without mentioning the part crime had played in the catastrophe, or the presence of a band of convicts in the country. Ayrton alone was informed of it. Then the little troop crossed the railway some yards above the bridge, and went on its way eastward.

CHAPTER XI.

FIRST PRIZE FOR GEOGRAPHY.

 CHAIN of hills lay on the horizon, and bounded the plain two miles from the railway. The waggon wound along the side of one, and came to a charming country, where fine trees grew in isolated groups, with quite tropical exuberance. Amongst the most admirable was the "casuarinas," which seems to have borrowed its robust structure of trunk from the oak, its odorous pods from the acacia, and its rough leaves from the pine. There grew the " banksia latifolia," with its curious and elegant cones, and large shrubs with falling twigs, looking like cascades of green water.

The little troop halted for an instant. Lady Glenarvan had asked Ayrton to stop his team. The large wheels of the waggon ceased to creak over the sand. Long green carpets extended under the groups of trees, but this grass was raised into regular mounds like a vast chess-board. Paganel knew that it was a native cemetery; it was so cool and shaded, made so gay by the birds, that it awoke no sad thought. It might have been one of the gardens of Eden before death was known, and seemed made for the living. But these graves, which the savage keeps in repair so piously, were already disappearing under a rising tide of verdure. Conquest had driven the Australian far from the land where his ancestors were resting, and colonisation would soon give up these fields of death to its flocks and herds. These native cemeteries have become rare; how many, trodden under foot by indifferent travellers, cover a quite recent generation!

In the meantime, Paganel and Robert, going before their companions, wound in and out of the shady alleys amongst the graves. They were talking and instructing one another, for the geographer pretended that he gained much in his conversations with Robert Grant. But they had not gone a quarter of a mile before Glenarvan saw them stop, then dismount, and look down on the ground. They appeared to be examining some very curious object.

Ayrton pricked his team, and the waggon soon reached the two friends. The cause of their halt and their astonishment was immediately seen. A native child, a little boy about eight years old, clothed in European garments, was sleeping peacefully in the shade of a magnificent banksia. His woolly hair, almost black skin, flat nose, thick lips, and very long arms, classed him immediately amongst the natives of the interior. But his physiognomy was intelligent, and it was certain that education had done something for this young savage.

Lady Glenarvan felt much interested; she got out of the waggon, and soon all the troop surrounded the little native, who was sleeping profoundly.

"Poor child!" said Mary Grant; "can he be lost in this desert?"

"I suppose," answered Lady Glenarvan, "he must have come some distance to visit this cemetery. Those he loved are, doubtless, buried here."

"But we must not leave him!" said Robert. "He is alone, and——"

Robert's charitable speech was interrupted by a

movement of the young native, who turned over without waking ; but then the surprise of each was extreme at seeing on his shoulders a board, on which was the following inscription :—

TOLINÉ,
PASSENGER TO ECHUCA,
CARE OF JEFFRIES SMITH, RAILWAY PORTER
PREPAID.

" Just like Englishmen !" cried Paganel. " They send a child like a parcel. They told me such a thing was done, but I would not believe it."

" Poor little fellow!" said Helena. " Was he in the train that ran off the line at Camden Bridge? Perhaps his parents were killed, and he is alone in the world !"

" I do not think so, Lady Glenarvan," answered John Mangles. " The address on his back shows that he was travelling alone."

" He is waking up," said Mary Grant.

The boy opened his eyes, and the light made him shut them again immediately. But Lady Glenarvan took his hand ; he got up and looked at the travellers with astonishment. He seemed frightened at first, but Helena's presence reassured him.

" Do you understand English, my boy ?" asked the young lady.

" Yes, I understand it and speak it," answered the child with a strong foreign accent, very much like that of French people speaking English.

" What is your name ?" asked Helena.

" Toliné," answered the little native.

" Ah ! Toliné!" cried Paganel. " If I am not

mistaken, Toliné means bark of a tree in Australian ?"

Toliné made an affirmative sign, and looked again at the ladies.

"Where do you come from, dear ?" asked Helena.

"From Melbourne, by the Sandhurst railway."

"Were you in the train that ran off the line at Camden ?" asked Lord Glenarvan.

"Yes, sir," answered Toliné, "but the God of the Bible protected me."

"Were you travelling alone ?"

"Yes, sir. The Reverend Mr. Paxton had asked Jeffries Smith to take care of me, but the poor porter was killed."

"Then you knew no one else in the train ?"

"No, sir; but God watches over children, and never deserts them."

Toliné said these things in a gentle voice that was very touching. When he spoke of God he grew serious, and his eyes lighted up. This religious enthusiasm in so young a child is easily explained. This boy was one of the young natives baptised by the English missionaries, and brought up by them as Methodists. His calm answers, neat appearance, and sober costume, already made him look like a little Wesleyan minister. But where was he going across these desert regions, and why had he left Camden Bridge ? Lady Glenarvan asked him these questions.

"I was going back to my tribe in the Lachlan," answered he. "I want to see my family again."

"Are they Australians ?" asked John Mangles.

"Yes, Lachlan Australians," answered Toliné.

"Have you a father and a mother?" said Robert Grant.

"Yes, my brother," answered Toliné, offering his hand to young Grant, who, touched at being called "brother," kissed the young native and made friends with him at once.

In the meantime the travellers, who were much interested by the answers of the young savage, had gradually seated themselves round him to listen. The sun was already going down behind the large trees. The place seemed favourable for a halt, and it did not much matter about going a few miles more before nightfall, so Glenarvan gave orders to have everything prepared for encamping. Ayrton unyoked the oxen; with the help of Mulrady and Wilson, he put clogs on them, and let them graze at will. The tent was set up. Olbinett prepared the meal. Toliné accepted the invitation to partake of it, not without ceremony, although he was hungry. They sat down to table, the two children side by side. Robert chose the best pieces for his new companion, and Toliné accepted them with timid yet charming grace.

Conversation did not flag; they all asked the boy questions, and wanted to know his history. It was very simple. His past was that of those poor natives confided, from their tenderest infancy, to the care of charitable societies, by the tribes in the neighbourhood of the colonies. The Australians have gentle manners. They do not profess towards their invaders the same ferocious hatred that characterises the New Zealanders, and perhaps some tribes of North Australia. They are frequently seen in the large towns, Adelaide, Sydney, and Melbourne, even in their primitive costume. They carry on a trade in the small objects of their industry hunting and fishing implements; some of the chiefs, doubtless for economy's sake, allow their children to profit by the offer of an English education. Toliné's parents, veritable savages of Lachlan, a vast region situated beyond the Murray, had done this. During the five years he had been at Melbourne he had never seen his parents, and yet the imperishable family sentiment was still alive in him, and it was to see his tribe, perhaps dispersed, and his family, perhaps destroyed, that he had taken the desert route.

"When you have seen your parents, shall you go back to Melbourne, my child?" asked Lady Glenarvan.

"Yes, ma'am," answered Toliné, looking at her affectionately.

"What do you mean to do when you are grown up?"

"I mean to help my brothers out of their misery and ignorance, and teach them to know and love God! I shall be a missionary."

The words, pronounced with animation by a child of eight, might make scoffers laugh, but they were understood and respected by these grave Scotch people. They admired the religious valour of the young disciple, already ready for the fight. Paganel was greatly moved, and felt real sympathy for the little native. For—must it be said?—this savage in a European dress had not pleased him much. He did not come to Australia to see the natives in top-coats. He did not want them to wear anything but their tattoo marks. This "respectable" costume confused his ideas. But from the time that Toliné spoke so enthusiastically, he revoked his opinion and became his admirer.

The end of this conversation was destined to make

the brave geographer the best friend of the little Australian. In answer to a question of Lady Glenarvan's, Toliné answered that he went to the Melbourne National School.

"What do you learn there?" asked Helena.

"The Bible, mathematics, geography."

"Ah, geography!" cried Paganel, touched in a sensitive place.

"Yes, sir," answered Toliné. "I had the first prize for geography before the Christmas holidays."

"You had a prize for geography, my boy?"

"Here it is, sir," said Toliné, taking a book out of his pocket.

It was a well-bound Bible. On the first page was written :—"*Melbourne National School, 1st prize for geography, Toliné, from Lachlan.*"

Paganel was delighted. An Australian native, who knew geography, was marvellous; he ought to have known, however, that this fact is not rare in Australian schools. The young savages are very apt at acquiring geographical knowledge, though they do not take to arithmetic in the same way. Lady Glenarvan explained to Toliné that Paganel was a celebrated geographer and a distinguished professor.

"A teacher of geography!" answered Toliné. "Oh, sir, question me."

"Question you, my boy?" said Paganel. "That I will. I meant to do it before you asked me. I shall not be sorry to see how geography is taught in the *Melbourne National School!*"

Then fixing his spectacles on his nose, and drawing up his long figure, he began his questions in his most professor-like tone.

" Toliné," said he, " stand up !"

Toliné, who was standing already, awaited in a modest position the questions of the geographer.

" Toliné," continued Paganel, " what are the five great divisions of the globe ?"

" Oceania, Asia, Africa, America, and Europe," answered Toliné.

" Perfect. We will first speak of Oceania, as we are in it now. What are its principal divisions ?"

" Malaysia, or the Indian Archipelago, Australia, and Polynesia. Its principal islands are Australia, which belongs to the English, New Zealand, which belongs to the English, Tasmania, which belongs to the English, Chatham, Auckland, Macquarie, Kermadec, Makin, Maraki, &c., which belong to the English."

" Good," answered Paganel; " but New Caledonia, the Sandwich Islands, the Mindanao, and the Pomotou ?"

" They are islands placed under the protection of Great Britain."

" How ! under the protection of Great Britain !" cried Paganel. " I thought it was France——"

" France !" said the little boy, looking astonished.

" *Tiens ! tiens !*" said Paganel; " so that is what they teach you at the *Melbourne National School ?*"

" Yes, sir. Is it not right ?"

" Oh, yes, perfect," answered Paganel. " All Oceania belongs to the English, that is an understood thing ! We will go on."

Paganel seemed half vexed, half surprised, much to the major's amusement.

" We will pass on to Asia now," said the geographer.

G

"Asia," answered Toliné, " is an immense country. Capital—Calcutta. Principal towns—Bombay, Madras, Calicut, Aden, Malacca, Singapore, Pegou, Colombo. Islands—The Laccadives, the Maldives, &c., &c., belonging to the English."

"Good! good! Toliné. And Africa?"

Africa contains two principal colonies. On the south, Cape Colony, with Cape Town for capital; and on the west, the English settlements; principal town, Sierra Leone."

"Well answered!" said Paganel. "It is useless to speak of Algeria or Egypt; they will not be in the Britannic atlas! We will pass on to America."

"America," answered Toliné, "is divided into North and South America. The former belongs to the English through Canada, New Brunswick, Nova Scotia; and the United States, under the administration of the Governor Johnson!"

" Governor Johnson!" cried Paganel, "the successor of the great and good Lincoln, assassinated by a madman, fanatic of slavery! Perfect! As to South America and the East Indies, with their Guiana, Jamaica, Trinidad, &c., they belong to the English, too. I shall not dispute the fact. But, Toliné, I should like to know what you, or rather your professors, have to say about Europe?"

" Europe?" answered Toliné, who understood nothing of the geographer's animation.

"Yes, Europe. To whom does Europe belong?"

" Why, Europe belongs to the English, of course!" answered the child.

"I thought as much," answered Paganel. "But how? That is what I want to know."

"Through England, Scotland, Ireland, Malta, the Channel Islands, the Hebrides, the Shetland Islands——"

"Good, Toliné; but there are other countries you have forgotten to mention."

"What countries, sir?" asked the child, nowise disconcerted.

"Spain, Russia, Austria, Prussia, France."

"They are provinces, not countries," said Toliné.

"*Par exemple!*" cried the Frenchman, snatching off his spectacles.

"Spain, capital Gibraltar," said Toliné.

"Admirable! perfect! sublime! And France, for I am a Frenchman, and should be glad to know to whom I belong?"

"France," answered Toliné, quietly, "is an English province, and Calais is the capital."

"Calais!" cried Paganel; "do you believe that Calais still belongs to England?"

"Of course."

"And that it is the capital of France?"

"Yes, sir, that is where the governor, Lord Napoleon, resides."

At these last words Paganel roared with laughter. Toliné did not know what to think of it. They had questioned him, and he had answered to the best of his ability. But the singularity of his answers could not be imputed to him; he did not know they were singular. However, he did not seem disconcerted, and waited gravely till Paganel had done laughing.

"I thought Toliné would teach you something you did not know before," said the major, laughing.

"He has indeed, major. So that is how they teach

geography at Melbourne! Europe, Asia, Africa,
America, Oceania, all the world belongs to the English.
With such an education as that, I understand the sub-
mission of the natives! Well, Toliné, and the moon,
does that belong to the English, too?"

" It will belong to them some day," gravely answered
the young savage.

Thereupon Paganel got up. He could not keep still,
and went a quarter of a mile from the encampment to
have his laugh out.

In the meantime Glenarvan had been to fetch a
book from his little travelling library. It was Richardson's " Geography."

" Here, my boy," said he to Toliné, " take this book;
you have some false ideas about geography, which it
will correct. I give it to you as a remembrance of our
meeting."

Toliné took the book without answering; he looked
it attentively, shaking his head with an air of incredulity,
without making up his mind to put it in his pocket.

Night was now come. It was ten o'clock. Robert
offered his friend Toliné the half of his bed, and the
little native accepted. A few moments afterwards
Lady Glenarvan and Mary Grant went back to their
compartment in the waggon, and the travellers lay
down under the tent, whilst Paganel's laughter rang
in chorus with the low, soft song of the wild magpie.

The next morning, when at six o'clock a ray of sunlight awoke the sleepers, they looked in vain for the
Australian child. Toliné had disappeared. Was his disappearance owing to his wish to get to the Lachlan
districts as quickly as possible, or had Paganel's
laughter offended him? No one knew.

But when Lady Glenarvan awoke she found on her breast a fresh bunch of leaves from the sensitive plant, and Paganel, in his coat pocket, discovered Richardson's "Geography!"

CHAPTER XII.

THE MINES OF ALEXANDER MOUNT.

IN 1814, Sir Roderick Impey Murchison, president of the Royal Geographical Society of London, found, by studying their conformation, remarkable points of resemblance between the chain of the Oural and the chain which runs from north to south, not far from the southern coast of Australia. The Oural being an auriferous chain, the learned geographer asked himself if the precious metal might not be met with in the Australian chain. He was not mistaken. In fact, two years before some specimens of gold had been sent to New South Wales, and had caused the emigration of a great number of Cornish miners to the auriferous regions of New Holland.

After that, miners flocked thither from all points of the globe—Englishmen, Americans, Italians, French, Germans, and Chinese. However, it was not until the 3rd of April, 1851, that Mr. Hargraves met with very rich gold beds, and offered to tell the Governor of Sydney, Sir Charles Fitz-Roy, where they were situated, for the modest sum of £500.

His offer was not accepted, but the news of the discovery had travelled far and wide. The diggers spread

ᴏver Summerhill and Leni's Pond. The town of Ophir
was founded, and soon justified its Biblical name.

Till then there had been no gold found in Victoria,
but a few months later, in August, 1851, the first gold
beds were discovered, and soon four districts were in
full activity. These were Ballarat, Ovens, Bendigo,
and Mount Alexander, all very rich; but on Ovens
river the abundance of water made the work difficult;
at Ballarat, an unequal distribution of the gold often
baffled the calculations of the diggers; at Bendigo the
ground was difficult; at Mount Alexander all the con-
ditions of success were united on even ground, and its
precious metal attained the highest price in the markets
of the entire world.

It was precisely to this place, so fruitful in fatal
ruins and unhoped-for fortunes, that the 37th parallel
was conducting the travellers.

After having marched the whole of the day on the
31st of December along a hilly road, that had fatigued
oxen and horses, they perceived the rounded summits
of Mount Alexander. They encamped in a narrow
gorge of this little chain, and the animals were allowed
to seek their food amongst the blocks of quartz scat-
tered over the ground. It was not till the next day,
the first of the year 1866, that the waggon made its
ruts on the roads of this opulent country.

Jacques Paganel and his companions were delighted
to see this celebrated mountain, called Geboor in the
native language. About eleven o'clock they reached
the digging centre. There exists a veritable town, with
workshops, banking-houses, church, barracks, cottages,
and newspaper offices. There are hotels, farms,
villas, and even a theatre. at ten shillings a place,

much frequented. They were then playing, with great success, a play called *Francis Obadiah, or the Fortunate Digger.* At the end the hero, in despair, puts in the spade for the last time, and finds an enormous nugget.

Glenarvan wished to see the gold-diggings, and so let the waggon go on before him under the care of Ayrton and Mulrady. He meant to rejoin it a few hours later. Paganel was enchanted with this determination, and as usual he made himself guide and cicerone of the little troop.

Following his advice, they went first to the bank. The streets were wide, macadamised, and carefully watered. Gigantic placards of the Gold Company (limited), the Digger's General Office, or the Nugget's Union, were hung about. The noise of machines, washing the sand and pulverising the precious quartz, filled the air.

Beyond the habitations stretched the "placers"—that is to say, large tracts of ground given up to the diggings. There miners were at work, engaged and well paid by the different companies. The ground was covered with holes, and the spades of the army of diggers glittered in the sun. They were men of all nations, not quarrelling, but accomplishing their task like paid workmen. The association of arms and capital had been substituted for the isolated action of the miner.

"There are some of the feverish searchers left," said Paganel. "I know that most of them let their arms to the companies, and are obliged to do so, for the auriferous ground is either let or sold by the Government. But there is one scheme left for those who can neither hire nor buy."

"What is that?" asked Helena.

"The chance of 'jumping,'" answered Paganel. "We, who have no right over these placers, we might, with plenty of luck, make a fortune."

"But how?" asked the major.

"By jumping, as I told you before."

"What is jumping?" asked the major again.

"It is an agreement entered into by the miners, which is often the cause of violence and disorder, but which the authorities have never been able to abolish."

"Go on, Paganel," said MacNabbs; "you are making our mouths water."

"It is agreed that any of this ground which has not been worked for twenty-four hours, holidays excepted, becomes public property. Whoever takes possession of it may dig and become rich, if he is lucky. So, Robert, my boy, if you find one of these neglected holes, it is yours."

"M. Paganel," said Mary Grant, "do not put such ideas into my brother's head."

"I was joking, Miss Mary," answered Paganel, "and Robert knows that. He a miner! Never! To dig the ground for the sake of a harvest is one thing, and to dig it for a little gold is another, and a wretched one, and one must be abandoned by God and man to do it."

After having visited the principal placers, and looked at the soil that was to be carried away, composed of quartz, clay, slate, and sand, the travellers arrived at the bank.

It was a vast edifice, with the national flag hanging from its summit. Lord Glenarvan was received by the general inspector, who did the honours of the place. It is there that the companies deposit the gold, for which they get a receipt. The time was far off when

the first diggers were taken advantage of by the traders
of the colony. They paid fifty-three shillings an ounce
for what they sold at sixty-five in Melbourne. The
trader, it is true, had the risks of transport, and as
highway robbers were plentiful, the escort did not
always arrive at its destination. Curious specimens of
gold were shown to the visitors, and the inspector gave
them curious details about the different ways of working
this metal. It is found generally under two forms, as
ore mixed with alluvian earth, or in quartz. According
to the nature of the ground, it is dug for or sought
on the surface. The latter is found in the beds of
torrents, or where they have washed it down in valleys
or ravines. The other is dug out of the slaty layers of
rock.

The visitors, after having looked at the different
specimens of gold, went over the mineral museum of
the bank. They saw all the products of Australian
soil ticketed and classified. Gold is not its only wealth ;
it may be compared to a vast casket, where nature
keeps her most precious jewels. In the glass-cases
shone the white topaz, the rival of Brazilian topazes,
the garnet, rubies, sapphires, and last, though not
least, diamonds. Nothing was wanting to complete this
collection of precious stones, and the gold was there to
set them in.

After they left the bank, they went back to the placers,
and there Paganel made his companions laugh by the
way he kept his eyes on the ground, picking up a pebble
here, a piece of quartz there, examining them with
attention, and then throwing them down in disgust.

"Have you lost anything, Paganel?" asked the
major.

"Yes," said Paganel, "we have always lost what we have not found in a country of precious stones. I don't know why I should like to carry off a nugget weighing a few ounces, or even twenty pounds, not more."

"What should you do with it?" said Glenarvan.

"Oh, I should present it to my country. I should deposit in the bank of France——"

"Which would accept it?"

"Certainly, under the form of railway stock."

Paganel was congratulated on the way he intended offering his nugget to his country, and Lady Glenarvan hoped he would find one worth having.

After a two-hours' walk, Paganel saw a decent-looking inn, and proposed that they should sit down there till it was time to go back to the waggon. Lady Glenarvan consented, and as it would not be an inn without refreshments, Paganel asked the landlord to serve some drink of the country. They brought a "nobler" for each person. The nobler is a glass of grog, but made in the opposite way to the British method. Instead of putting a small glass of brandy into a large glass of water, they put a small glass of water into a large glass of brandy. It was rather too Australian, and, to the great astonishment of the landlord, a large decanter of water was added to the nobler, which thus was British grog again.

CHAPTER XIII.

AUSTRALIAN AND NEW ZEALAND GAZETTE.

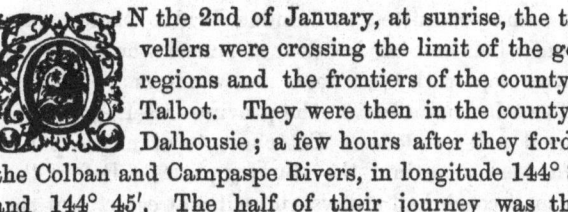N the 2nd of January, at sunrise, the travellers were crossing the limit of the gold regions and the frontiers of the county of Talbot. They were then in the county of Dalhousie; a few hours after they forded the Colban and Campaspe Rivers, in longitude 144° 35′ and 144° 45′. The half of their journey was then accomplished. Another fortnight as happily passed would find the little troop on the shores of Twofold Bay.

They were all well. Paganel's promises about the healthiness of the climate were realised. There was little or no humidity, and the heat was not too great. A single modification had been made in the order of march since Camden Bridge. When Ayrton knew about the crime on the railway he took some precautions which had hitherto been useless. The sportsmen were not to lose sight of the waggon. Some one was always to be on guard during the hours of encampment. All the arms were to be reloaded morning and evening. It was certain that there was a band of malefactors abroad, and though there was nothing to cause immediate fear, it was well to be prepared for anything. Needless to add that these precautions were taken without the knowledge of Lady Glenarvan and Mary Grant, whom Glenarvan did not wish to frighten. The travellers were not alone in taking precautions against the convicts. In isolated hamlets and stations the inhabitants and squatters closed their houses at nightfall.

Dogs were set free in the inclosure, who barked at every approaching footstep. The shepherds on horseback, who reassembled their cattle to bring them in for the night, carried a rifle at their saddle-bow. The news of the crime committed at Camden Bridge made many a colonist bolt and bar his door at sunset who before had always slept with open doors and windows.

The administration of the province itself gave proof of zeal and prudence. Detachments of native policemen were sent into the country places. Before then the mail-coach had always run without escort, but that day, as Glenarvan's troop was crossing the road from Kilmore to Heatcote, the mail galloped past in a cloud of dust, but not too quickly for Glenarvan to see the rifles of the mounted policemen who accompanied it. It seemed like going back to the fatal time when the discovery of the first gold threw the scum of European populations on to the Australian continent.

One mile after the waggon entered the first forest that the travellers had seen since they left Cape Bernouilli. The sight of the eucalyptus evoked a cry of admiration; they were 200 feet high, their spongy bark was five inches thick, and their trunks, trickling with odorous resin, measured twenty feet round, and were 150 high. They were straight and smooth, and looked like so many columns. At the top they spread out into gyrose branches, with alternate leaves at their extremity, and a single flower, with a chalice like an inverted urn.

Under this green sky the air circulated freely; incessant ventilation absorbed the humidity of the ground; horses, oxen, and waggon could pass comfortably between these trees, which made a very different forest to

those where a way has to be cut through by pioneers.
A carpet of grass at the feet of the trees, a cloth of
verdure at their summits, long perspectives of columns,
but little shade and coolness, a special light like that
through transparent tissues, all constituted a strange
spectacle, rich in new effects. The forest of the Oceanian
continent is nothing like the forests of the New World.
If the shade is not great nor the obscurity profound
under these domes of verdure, it is because these trees
present a curious anomaly in the disposition of their
leaves. They turn sideways to the sun, and the light
streams through them to the ground, as through the
laths of a Venetian blind. All the travellers remarked
this singularity, and Paganel was asked the reason of it.

"What astonishes me here," said he, "is not the
singularity of nature — nature knows what she is
about—but botanists do not always know what they are
talking about. Nature has not made a mistake in
giving a special kind of foliage to these trees, but men
have in calling them ' eucalyptus.' "

"What does the word mean?" asked Mary Grant.

"It comes from εὖ καλύπτω, and means ' *I cover well.*'
They took care to make the mistake in Greek, so that it
should not be so apparent, but it is evident that the
eucalyptus covers badly."

"Granted, Paganel," answered Glenarvan. "Now
tell us why the leaves grow like that."

"For a purely physical reason," answered Paganel.
"In this country, where the air is dry, rain is rare, and
the ground dry, trees have no need either of sun or air.
Humidity failing, sap fails too. The leaves are made
narrow to preserve them from being too rapidly evapo-
rated by the sun. That is why they turn their profile

to its light. There is nothing more intelligent than a
leaf."

"And nothing more selfish!" added the major.
"These only think of themselves, and not at all of
travellers."

They were all of MacNabbs' opinion except Paganel
who, even while wiping his forehead, congratulated
himself on marching under trees without shade. However it is to be regretted, nothing protects the traveller
against the heat in these forests, which often take a
long time to cross.

During the whole of that day the waggon rolled on
amongst the eucalyptus. It met neither an animal nor
a native. In the evening they encamped at the foot of
one of the giant trees that bore marks of a recent fire.
It was like a tall factory chimney, for the flame had
hollowed it out from top to bottom. This custom of
the squatters and natives will end by destroying these
magnificent trees, and they will disappear like the
cedars of Lebanon. Olbinett, following Paganel's advice,
lighted his fire for supper in this tubular trunk; it
drew well, and the smoke was lost amongst the foliage.
They took the necessary precaution for the night, and
Ayrton, Mulrady, Wilson, and John Mangles took it
in turns to watch till daybreak.

During the whole day of January 3rd, the long
avenues of the interminable forest stretched on before
the travellers, who thought they were never going to
end. However, towards evening, the trees were not so
thick, and a few miles off, in a little plain, appeared an
agglomeration of regular houses.

"Seymour!" cried Paganel; "that is the last town
we shall meet with before leaving Victoria."

"Is it important?" asked Helena.

"It is a simple parish," answered Paganel, "and is on its way to be a municipality."

"Shall we find a decent hotel there?" asked Glenarvan.

"I hope so," answered the geographer.

"Well, we will enter the town. I daresay the ladies will not be sorry to stay a night there."

"No," said Helena, "unless it will cause any inconvenience or delay."

"It will not," answered Glenarvan. "The oxen and horses are tired; to-morrow we will set out again at daybreak."

It was nine o'clock. Darkness was gradually setting in. All the troop entered the wide streets of Seymour under the direction of Paganel, who always seemed to know perfectly what he had never seen. But his instinct guided him, and he went straight to Campbell's North British Hotel. Horses and oxen were taken to the stables, the waggon put under a shed, and the travellers conducted to pretty comfortable rooms. At ten o'clock they were all seated round the supper table. Paganel had just come in from going round the town with Robert, and related his adventures very laconically. He had seen nothing whatever.

A less absent-minded man would have remarked some agitation in the streets of Seymour; groups were gathered here and there, getting gradually larger; people were talking at their house-doors, and questioning one another in evident anxiety. The evening papers were being read aloud and commented upon. These symptoms could not escape the least attentive observer, and yet Paganel had seen nothing.

The major, without going so far, without even going out of the hotel, heard the news that agitated the little town. Ten minutes' conversation with the loquacious Dickson, the landlord of the inn, informed him. But he did not say a word about it. It was not until the supper was over, and the ladies and Robert had gone to bed, that the major said to his companions—

"They have found out who committed the crime on the Sandhurst railway."

"Are they arrested?" asked Ayrton, quickly.

"No," answered the major, without appearing to notice the quartermaster's eagerness—eagerness justified by the circumstance.

"That is a pity," added Ayrton.

"Well," asked Glenarvan, "to whom do they attribute the crime?"

"Read," answered the major, handing Glenarvan a copy of the *Australian and New Zealand Gazette*, "and you will see that the inspector of police was not mistaken."

Glenarvan read that, according to the coroner's inquest at Camden Bridge, the crime was attributed to a band of convicts escaped six months before from Perth station, in West Australia, as they were being transferred to Norfolk Island. The band was composed of twenty-nine convicts, commanded by a certain Ben Joyce, a most dangerous malefactor, who had arrived in Australia some months before, it was not known by what ship, and whom justice had never been able to seize.

When Glenarvan had finished, MacNabbs turned to the geographer and said—

"You see, Paganel, there are convicts in Australia."

"Escaped convicts, yes, that is evident," answered Paganel; "but there are none regularly admitted. Those fellows had no right to be here."

"Right or not, here they are," answered Glenarvan. "The question is, ought their presence to modify our plans and stop our journey. What do you think, John?"

The captain did not answer immediately; he hesitated between the grief it would cause the two children to abandon the search for their father and the fear of compromising the expedition.

"If Lady Glenarvan and Miss Grant were not with us," he said, "I should care very little for this band of convicts."

Glenarvan understood him, and answered—

"Of course there is no question of giving up the search; but perhaps it would be prudent to rejoin the Duncan at Melbourne, and then go east on the track of Captain Grant. What do you think, MacNabbs?"

"I should like to know Ayrton's opinion before I decide," answered the major.

The quartermaster, directly addressed, looked at Glenarvan.

"I think," said he, "that we are 200 miles from Melbourne, and that the danger, if it exists, is as great on the route to the south as the east. Both are little frequented; one is as good as the other. Besides, I do not think eight well-armed and resolute men need fear a band of thirty malefactors."

"Well spoken, Ayrton," answered Paganel. "By going on we might discover some traces of Captain Grant, which we should not do if we went southwards.

I am of your opinion, and think these convicts are not worth bestowing a thought upon."

Thereupon the proposition to change nothing in the programme of their journey was put to the vote.

"My lord," said Ayrton, as they were going to separate for the night, "would it not be opportune to send word to the Duncan to join you on the east coast?"

"What would be the use?" asked Mangles. "It will be time to send the order when we get to Twofold Bay. If anything forced us to go to Melbourne, we might regret that we had sent the Duncan away from there. Besides, the damage she sustained cannot be repaired yet. I think we had better wait."

"Very well," said Ayrton, who did not insist.

The next day the little troop, armed and ready for any event, left Seymour, and, half an hour afterwards, again entered the forest of eucalyptus.

Glenarvan would have preferred to travel in open country, where ambushes would not be so practicable, but there was no choice, and the waggon wound all day amongst the tall, monotonous trees. In the evening, after crossing the northern frontier of the county of Anglesey and the 146th meridian, they encamped on the verge of the Murray district.

CHAPTER XIV.

THE MAJOR'S MONKEYS.

HE next morning, January 5th, the travellers set foot on the vast Murray territory. Civilisation has not yet divided it into distinct counties. It is the least known and least frequented of the province. Its forests will one day fall under the axe of the bushman; its meadows be given up to the flocks and herds of the squatter; but at present it is virgin soil, and the same as it emerged from the Indian Ocean.

This territory bears a significative name on English maps, that of "Reserve for the Blacks." It is there that the natives have been brutally thrust back by the colonists. They have left them in distant plains, under inaccessible woods, certain places where the native races will drag out the short remaining period of their miserable existence. Any white man, colonist, emigrant, squatter, or bushman, may cross the limit of these preserves—the black alone must never leave them.

"Fifty years ago," said Paganel, as he rode along, "we should have met with many tribes of natives along our route, and as yet we have not met with one. In another century there will not be a black left."

In fact, the preserve seemed to be quite deserted, and not a trace of an encampment or a hut was to be seen. Plains and woods succeeded one another, and by degrees the country began to look wild. It seemed as if no living thing, either man or animal, frequented these distant regions, when Robert, stopping before a copse of eucalyptus, cried out—

"A monkey! there is a monkey!" And he pointed to a large black body which was gliding from branch to branch with surprising agility; it passed from one tree to another, as if sustained in the air by some membranous apparatus. In this strange country, did monkeys fly, like certain foxes to whom Nature had given bat's wings?

The waggon stopped, and they all watched the animal, which gradually disappeared in the top of the eucalyptus. Soon they saw it descend with the rapidity of lightning, run along the ground with a thousand contortions, and then seize with its long arms the smooth trunk of an enormous gum-tree. They wondered how it was going to climb the straight, slippery trunk which it could not encircle. But the monkey made little notches in it with a sort of axe, and, by stepping on them, reached the branches; in a few seconds it had disappeared amongst the foliage.

"What sort of a monkey can that be?" exclaimed the major.

"That monkey," answered Paganel, "is an Australian, *pur sang!*"

The companions of the geographer had not time to shrug their shoulders when cries of "Coo-eeh! cooeeh!" were heard at a little distance. Ayrton pricked his oxen, and, a hundred paces farther, the travellers found themselves in a native encampment.

The spectacle was a sad one. About a dozen tents stood on the naked ground. These "gunyos," made with strips of bark, only sheltered their miserable inhabitants on one side. These beings, degraded by misery, were repulsive-looking objects. There were about thirty of them, men, women, and children, clothed in kangaroo-skins, which hung in rags. Their first movement on seeing the waggon was to fly; but a few words from Ayrton, pronounced in an unintelligible jargon, seemed to reassure them. They then came timidly back like animals to whom some tempting piece of meat is offered.

These natives, from five feet four inches to five feet seven inches high, were the colour of soot, had flaky hair, long arms, prominent stomachs, and hairy bodies; covered with tattoo marks and scars from the cuts they inflicted upon themselves in their funeral ceremonies. Nothing could be more horrible than their monstrous faces, enormous mouths, flat noses, and prominent lower jaws, armed with white but projecting teeth. No other human creatures present a type so purely animal.

"Robert was not mistaken," said the major, "they are monkeys—*pur sang*, if you like—but certainly monkeys."

"Cousin," said Lady Glenarvan, gently, "do you think it right, then, that they should be hunted like wild beasts? The poor things are men!"

"Men!" cried MacNabbs. "At the best they are only intermediary between men and ourang-outangs! I am sure, if I measured their facial angle, I should find it as small as a monkey's."

MacNabbs was right there. The facial angle of the Australian is very sharp, and, like the ourang-outang's, measures sixty to sixty-two degrees. It was not without reason that M. de Rienzi proposed to classify these poor creatures as "pithecomorphes"—that is to say, men in the form of monkeys.

Lady Glenarvan and Miss Grant had left the waggon,

and were offering food to the natives, who swallowed
it with repulsive greediness. The blacks might have
taken the charitable women for divinities, as their
religion teaches them that the blacks become white
after their death.

But it was the women who most excited the pity
of the two Englishwomen. Nothing is comparable to
their condition; nature has refused them the least
charm, they are slaves, and the only wedding present
they get are blows from the "waddie," a sort of stick
their masters constantly carry. They become prema-
turely old, and have all the painful work of their
wandering life to do; they not only have to carry their
children rolled up in a packet of willows, but the
hunting and fishing implements, and the provisions of
"phormium tenax," with which they make nets. They
procure the family food, catch lizards, opossums, and
serpents, sometimes at the summit of trees; cut the
wood for fuel, and the bark for the tents; poor beasts
of burden, they never rest, and only eat, after their
masters, the worst of the food.

At that moment some of these miserable creatures—
famishing, perhaps—were trying to catch birds by
offering them corn. They were lying on the scorching
ground as motionless as the dead, and had been waiting, perhaps for hours, till some bird came within reach
of their hands. This was the only trap they knew,
and none but Australian birds would ever let themselves be caught by it.

In the meantime the native men surrounded the
travellers, who were obliged to protect themselves
against their pillaging instincts. They speak a hissing
dialect, formed by clapping the tongue, which resembles

the cries of animals. Their voice, however, has often soft inflections; the word "nokie, nokie," often repeated, was accompanied by gestures that translated it to mean "give, give." They asked for everything. Olbinett had much to do to defend the luggage compartment, and especially the provisions. The poor, famished creatures looked imploringly at the contents of the waggon, and Glenarvan gave orders to distribute food to them. The natives understood him, and gave themselves up to demonstrations which would have moved the hardest heart. They roared like beasts in a menagerie when they receive their daily food.

Olbinett gave to the women first, but they dared not eat before their dreaded masters, who threw themselves upon the biscuit and dried meat like wild animals upon a prey.

When Mary Grant thought that, perhaps, her father was a prisoner amongst such natives, her eyes filled with tears. John Mangles, who was watching her with anxious attention, guessed the thoughts which filled her heart, and anticipated her wish by questioning the quartermaster of the Britannia.

"Ayrton," said he, "were the natives you were amongst like these?"

"Yes, captain," answered Ayrton. "All these tribes are alike. Only here you see but a handful, whilst on the banks of the Darling the tribes are numerous, and commanded by a powerful chief."

"But what can a European do amongst these natives?" asked Mangles.

"What I did myself," answered Ayrton. "He hunts and fishes with them, takes part in their wars, and, as I have already told you, is treated according to the services he can render; and if he is at all brave and intelligent, he holds a good position in the tribe."

"But he is a prisoner," said Mary.

"And is closely watched day and night," added Ayrton.

"However, you succeeded in making your escape Ayrton," said the major, taking a part in the conversation.

"Yes, Mr. MacNabbs; during a fight between my tribe and a neighbouring one I succeeded, and do not regret it. But if it had to be done again, I believe I should prefer eternal slavery to the tortures I endured in crossing the deserts of the interior. God keep the captain from attempting that means!"

"Yes, certainly," answered John Mangles, "we must hope, Miss Mary, that your father is kept prisoner by a native tribe. We shall find traces of him more easily than if he were wandering through the forests of the continent."

"You still hope, then?" asked the young girl.

"I hope one day to see you happy, Miss Mary, with God's help!"

Mary Grant's tearful eyes could alone thank the young captain.

During this conversation an unaccustomed commotion had occurred amongst the savages; they were shouting and running with their arms in their hands, seemingly in fury.

Glenarvan did not know what to think of it, when the major asked Ayrton what it meant, and added—

"As you have lived amongst the Australians, you, doubtless, know their language."

"Every tribe has a different idiom," answered the

quartermaster, " but I can make out that, out of gratitude, they are going to treat you to a sham fight."

The natives thereupon began the attack with well-
feigned fury — so well feigned, indeed, that, without
knowing it beforehand, it might have been taken for
reality. But Australians are excellent mimics, and on
that occasion they displayed remarkable talents.

Their instruments of attack and defence consist of a
club and a species of tomahawk, a very sharp stone
fixed between two sticks with gum. This axe has a
handle ten feet long. It is a formidable weapon of
war, and a useful instrument of peace; it brings down
branches and heads, and cuts away trees or bodies, according to circumstances.

All these arms were brandished in frantic hands
amidst the noise of vociferations. The combatants
threw themselves upon one another; some fell as if
dead; others uttered the victors' cry. The women,
especially the old ones, possessed with the demon of
war, excited them, threw themselves on the dead, and
mutilated them with a ferocity which could not have
been more horrible had it been real. The children,
amongst whom the little girls were the most fierce,
thumped each other with ferocious venom.

This sham fight had lasted about ten minutes when
the combatants suddenly stopped. The arms dropped
from their hands, and a profound silence succeeded the
tumult. The natives remained fixed in their last atti-
tude, as if petrified.

Why they had stopped was soon perceived. A flight
of cockatoos was at that moment flying over the
gum-trees. They were filling the air with their cries,
and the bright shades on their plumage made them

look like a flying rainbow. It was the appearance of this bright flight of birds that had interrupted the fight. One of the natives seized an instrument of a peculiar shape, painted red, left his still motionless companions, and crept amongst the trees and bushes towards the flock of cockatoos. He did this so noiselessly that he neither touched a leaf nor displaced a pebble. He moved about like a shadow.

When he had arrived at the proper distance, he threw his instrument in a horizontal line at two feet from the ground. It flew thus for a distance of about forty feet, then suddenly, without touching the ground, it sprang up at a right angle 100 feet in the air, struck a dozen birds mortally, and, describing a parabola, fell again at the feet of the native.

Glenarvan and his companions were struck dumb with astonishment; they could not believe their eyes.

"It is the 'boomerang,'" said Ayrton.

"The boomerang!" cried Paganel, "the Australian boomerang!"

And, like a child, he ran to pick up the marvellous instrument, to see "what was inside."

This boomerang consisted of a piece of hard bent wood, from thirty to forty inches long. It was about three inches thick in the middle, and its two extremities ended in sharp points. The convex side had two very sharp edges. It was as simple as it was incomprehensible.

"This, then, is the famous boomerang!" said Paganel, after having attentively examined the strange instrument. "Only a morsel of wood, and nothing more. What could make it spring up all at once from its horizontal course, and come back to the hand that

threw it ? Neither savants nor travellers have ever
given any explanation of this phenomenon."

"Is it not something like a hoop which, hurled in a
certain fashion, comes back to the point it started
from ?" said John Mangles.

"Or like a billiard-ball struck in a certain place ?"
added Glenarvan.

"Not at all," answered Paganel; "in both cases
there is a point of support which determines the re-
action—the ground for the hoop and the board for the
ball. But here there is none; the instrument does not
touch the ground, and yet it springs up to a considerable
height!"

"But how do you explain the fact, M. Paganel?"
asked Helena.

"I do not explain it at all; I only record it once
more; the effect is evidently due to the way the boomerang is hurled and its peculiar conformation. But
the way it is thrown still remains a secret of the
Australians."

"In any case, it is very ingenious—for monkeys,"
added Helena, looking at the major, who shook his
head in a very unconvinced manner.

In the meanwhile the time was going, and Glenarvan
thought he ought no longer to delay his march eastward; he was, therefore, going to beg the ladies to
go back to their waggon, when a savage ran up
to them, and pronounced some words with great
animation.

"They have perceived some cassowaries," said Ayrton.

"Do they mean to hunt them, then ?" asked Glenarvan.

"We must see that," cried Paganel. "It is certain

to be very curious   Perhaps they will use the boomerang."

"What do you think, Ayrton?"

"It will not take long, my lord," answered the
quartermaster.

The natives had not lost an instant.   It was a stroke
of good fortune for them to kill cassowaries.   The tribe
has provisions assured for several days.   Their hunters
use all their skill in the hunt.   But how, without guns,
were they going to bring down, and, without dogs, to
get at, so agile an animal?

The emu, or cassowary, called "moureuk" by the
natives, is an animal which begins to be rare in the plains
of Australia.   It is a large bird about two and a half feet
high, and has white flesh very much like that of the
turkey; its head has a horny covering, its eyes are light
brown, and its beak bent from top to bottom; its feet
have three toes, armed with powerful nails; its wings
are veritable stumps, and it cannot use them for flying;
its plumage is darker on the neck and chest.   But
although it does not fly, it can run and beat the fleetest
horse on the turf.   It can, therefore, only be taken
by stratagem.   That is why, at the call of the native,
ten Australians enrolled themselves into a band of
skirmishers in an admirable plain, where the indigo
grew wild, and made the ground blue with its flowers.
The travellers stopped on the borders of a wood of
mimosas.

At the approach of the natives half a dozen birds
rose, took flight, and alighted about a mile off.   When
the hunter of the tribe had marked their position, he
made a sign to his comrades to stop.   They lay down on
the ground, whilst he, drawing two cassowary skins skil-

fully sewn together from his net, put them on. He put his right arm above his head, imitating the movement of the bird seeking its food.

The native advanced towards the flock, sometimes stopping and pretending to peck grains, sometimes raising the dust with his feet. The stratagem was perfect, as nothing could be a more faithful reproduction. He arrived thus, imitating the cry of the birds, into the very midst of the flock, when he suddenly brandished his club, and five birds fell around him. The hunter had succeeded, and the hunt was over.

Then Glenarvan and his friends took leave of the natives, who showed little regret at the separation. Perhaps the success of their cassowary hunt had made them forget the satisfying of their excessive hunger. They had not even the gratitude of the stomach, more lively than that of the heart amongst savages and animals.

"Now, cousin," said Lady Glenarvan to the major, " you will agree that Australians are not monkeys."

"Because they can perfectly imitate an animal?" replied the major. "On the contrary, that justifies my doctrine."

"A joke is not an answer," said Helena. "You must acknowledge you were wrong."

"Well, then, yes, or rather, no. Australians are not monkeys, but monkeys are Australians. You remember what negroes affirm about the interesting race of ourang-outangs?"

"No, what?" asked Helena.

"They say that they do not speak because they will not work, at least so said a jealous negro about an ourang-outang that his master fed "

CHAPTER XV.

MILLIONAIRE CATTLE BREEDERS.

FTER a tranquil night passed in longitude 146° 15', the travellers, at six a.m., on January 6th, continued their journey across the vast district.   They twice crossed tracks of squatters going northwards, and then the different footprints would have got mixed but that Glenarvan's horse left the imprint of his Black Station shoes upon the plain.   They had to cross many temporary creeks which came down from the sides of the "Buffalo Ranges," a chain of hills whose picturesque outline undulated on the horizon.

They resolved to encamp there that evening.   Ayrton hurried on his team, and, after a day's journey of thirty-five miles, the oxen arrived rather fatigued.   The tent was set up under the large trees, night came, and supper was quickly despatched.   They thought less of eating than sleeping after such a journey.

Paganel, who took the first watch, gun on shoulder, marched up and down the encampment to keep himself awake.

Notwithstanding the absence of the moon, the night was nearly luminous under the light of the southern constellations.   The savant amused himself with reading the grand book of the firmament, so interesting to those who understand it.   He was thus more occupied with the sky than the earth, when a distant sound awoke him from his reverie.   He listened attentively, and, to his great astonishment, thought he recognised the sound of a piano; some arpeggio chords reached him; he could not mistake them.

"A piano in the desert!" said Paganel to himself. "I cannot admit that."

It was, in fact, very surprising, and Paganel liked rather to believe that some strange Australian bird was imitating the sounds of an Erard or a Broadwood than that he was listening to a production of their factories. But at that moment a clear voice was heard singing to the pianoforte accompaniment; Paganel listened without giving in to the evidence of his senses. A few moments after he was forced to recognise the sublime air that reached his ear—it was "Il mio tesoro tanto," from *Don Juan*.

"*Parbleu!*" exclaimed the Frenchman, "Australian birds may be musicians, but they cannot sing Mozart!"

Then he listened to the master's sublime inspiration till it was ended. The effect of the sweet melody in the still starlight night was indescribable. Paganel remained long under the charm of the music; then the voice stopped, and silence resumed its reign.

When Wilson came to relieve Paganel, he found him plunged in a profound reverie. Paganel said nothing to the sailor, he meant to tell Glenarvan about it the next morning.

They were awakened the following day by an unexpected barking outside the tent. Glenarvan immediately rose. Two magnificent pointers were coursing on the borders of a small wood. At the approach of the travellers they barked louder than ever.

"Can there be a station in this desert," said Glenarvan, " and sportsmen as well as their dogs?"

Paganel was just going to relate his impressions

of the previous night when two young men appeared, mounted on superb English hunters. They were clothed in elegant shooting costume, and stopped at the sight of the little troop encamped in their gipsy fashion. They seemed to be asking themselves what the presence of armed men in that neighbourhood meant, when they perceived the ladies descending from the waggon.

As soon as they were on the ground they went up to them, hat in hand. Glenarvan met them, and in his quality of stranger gave his name. The young men bowed, and the elder of the two said—

"My lord, will you and your companions do us the honour of resting a little in our house? We are Michael and Sandy Patterson, proprietors of Hottam Station. You are on the station land now, and have only a quarter of a mile to go."

"Gentlemen," answered Glenarvan, "we have no right to take advantage of your hospitality."

"By accepting it, my lord, you will oblige poor exiles only too glad to do the honours of the desert."

Glenarvan bowed in sign of consent.

'Sir," said Paganel, addressing Michael Patterson, "may I ask if you are the gentleman who was singing that divine air of Mozart's yesterday?"

"Yes, sir," answered the gentleman, "and my cousin Sandy was accompanying me."

"Well, sir," continued Paganel, "receive the sincere compliments of a Frenchman, and a passionate lover of music."

Then Michael Patterson pointed on the right to the route they were to follow. The horses were left to the care of Ayrton and the sailors, and the travellers, talk-

ing and admiring, went on foot with their young hosts
to the habitation of Hottam Station.

It was really a magnificent place, kept with the
rigorous severity of an English park. Immense meadows, surrounded by grey palisades, extended as far as
the eye could reach. There, oxen were grazing by
thousands and sheep by millions.

Long avenues of evergreen trees stretched in all
directions. Here and there were shrubberies of " grass-
trees," bushes ten feet high, similar to the dwarf-palm,
with long narrow leaves. The air was filled with the
scent of the mint-laurel; its white flowers, then in bloom,
gave out the finest aromatic perfume.

The transplanted productions of European climates
were mixed with the native trees. Peach, pear, apple,
fig, and orange-trees, even the oak, were recognised
with delight by the travellers, who saw birds in their
native trees they never knew before. Amongst others
the " satin-bird," with its soft plumage, and the " seri-
cules," clothed in gold and black velvet. They also
saw, for the first time, the lyre-bird, whose tail is
shaped like Orpheus' graceful instrument.

In the meantime Glenarvan was listening to the two
young Pattersons, who were telling him their history.
It was that of many young, intelligent, and industrious
Englishmen, who do not think that the possession of
riches exempts them from work. They were son and
nephew of a London banker. When they had attained
their majority, the banker said to them, " Here are so
many thousands, young men. Go to some distant
colony and make good use of them. Get experience of
life while you work. If you succeed, so much the better;
if you fail, there will be no great harm done. I shall

i

not regret a few thousands if they make men of you."
The two young men obeyed, and chose the colony of
Victoria, in Australia, wherein to found a settlement.
In less than three years it was as prosperous as heart
could desire. There are more than 3,000 stations in
Victoria, New South Wales, and South Australia; some
belong to squatters, who raise cattle, others to settlers,
whose principal industry is the cultivation of the soil.
Until the arrival of the two young Englishmen, the
largest settlement of this kind was that of Mr. Jamie-
son, on the Paroo, one of the tributaries of the
Darling.

The two young men were both squatters and settlers,
and Hottam Station was now the most considerable in
the country. It was situated at a great distance from
the principal towns, in the midst of the little-frequented
districts of the Murray. It occupied the space lying
between 146° 48′ and 147°—that is to say, a square
surface of nearly fifteen miles. It was well watered
by numerous creeks and tributaries of Oven's river,
which runs north into the bed of the Murray. The
raising of cattle and general farming succeeded there
admirably on 10,000 acres of well-cultivated land.

Michael and Sandy Patterson were giving the last of
these details when, at the extremity of an avenue of
"casuarinas," appeared the dwelling-house. It was a
charming place, built of wood and bricks, in the form
of a châlet, with a verandah, from which hung Chinese
lanterns. On the lawns and amongst the flower-beds
bronze candelabra supported elegant lanterns; at night
all this park was lighted with gas made from a little
gasometer hidden under thickets of arborescent ferns.

No out-houses were situated near the house. They

composed a village of twenty houses and huts, situated
a quarter of a mile off in a lone village. Telegraph
wires put this village and the house into instant communication.

The avenue was soon passed; a little iron bridge of
elegant construction gave access to the park; the doors
of the house were opened, and the guests of Hottam
Station were soon in the sumptuous apartment of their
hosts. All the luxury of artistic and fashionable
existence lay before them. They were shown through
a hall ornamented with sporting subjects into a large
drawing-room with five windows in it. There they
found a piano strewed over with classical and modern
music, easels with half-finished pictures on them, brackets
with marble statuettes, pictures of Flemish masters on
the walls, thick carpets, tapestries embroidered in
mythological subjects—in short, everything that could
recall the European comforts enjoyed by rich and cultivated people.

Lady Glenarvan walked to one of the windows and
was delighted with the view from it. The house was
on a hill side, and overlooked a wide valley which
stretched as far as the mountains on the east. Meadows,
woods, and hills " mixed in one another's arms," to one
pure image of delight. No other landscape in the
world could be compared to it, not even the renowned
Valley of Paradise on the Norwegian frontiers of Tele-
marck. The lovely scene changed with the shifting
tints made by the sunlight; it satisfied the utmost
dream the most brilliant imagination could form.

While they were lost in admiration, Sandy Patterson
had ordered breakfast, and, in less than a quarter of
an hour after their arrival at the station, the travellers

were seated before a sumptuous meal. The dishes and wines were of indisputable quality, but the best sauce was the evident pleasure of the two young hosts at being able to offer their splendid hospitality.

It was not long before they heard all about Glenarvan's expedition, in which they took a great interest, and gave great hope of success to Captain Grant's children.

"It is evident that Captain Grant is in the hands of the natives as he has not been heard of in the coast settlements," said Michael. "He must have been made prisoner directly he landed."

"That is precisely what happened to his quartermaster, Ayrton," answered John Mangles.

"Have you heard nothing about the shipwreck?" asked Helena of the two young men.

"Nothing," answered Michael.

"What sort of treatment do you think Captain Grant would receive from the natives?"

"The Australians are not cruel, Lady Glenarvan," answered the young squatter; "Miss Grant may make herself easy on that score. There are many examples of their gentle character, and Europeans have lived a long time amongst them without having to complain of their brutality."

"King, the only survivor of Burke's expedition, amongst others," said Paganel.

"Yes," said Sandy, "and an English soldier named Buckley, who deserted from Port Philip in 1803, and lived thirty-three years with the natives."

"Since then," added Michael, "I saw in one of the last numbers of the *Australian Gazette* that a man named Morrill has just been given up to his countrymen after sixteen years slavery. The same thing happened to him that must have happened to Captain Grant, for he was made prisoner by the natives after the wreck of the ship Peruvian in 1846."

These words of the young squatter gave new hopes to the members of the expedition, and delighted Mary and Robert.

After that they talked of the convicts, when the ladies had left the table. The young squatters knew about the catastrophe at Camden Bridge, but they felt no uneasiness about the band of escaped ruffians. They dared not attack a station in which, at least, a hundred workmen were employed. The young men thought it improbable that the convicts would adventure into the deserts of the Murray, where there was nothing for them to do, or into the New South Wales colonies, where the routes were well guarded. Such was Ayrton's opinion also.

Lord Glenarvan could not refuse his amiable young host's invitation to pass the day at Hottam Station. It would make a delay of twelve hours, which might be put to profitable use as a day of rest for the oxen and horses. When once the young men had received his assent, they submitted to their guests a programme for the day, which was accepted with pleasure.

At twelve o'clock seven vigorous hunters were pawing the ground before the doors of the house. An elegant break and four-in-hand were there for the ladies. For four hours they hunted in a park as large as some German states. It would have held Reuss-Schleitz or Saxe-Cobourg-Gotha. Game abounded. Robert did marvels by the side of Major MacNabbs; he was here, there, and everywhere, always the first to âre. But John Mangles watched over him, and re-assured Mary. They killed, during the battue, several animals peculiar to the country; amongst others, the "wombat" and the "bandicoot." The former is herbi-vorous, and burrows like the badger; it is as large as a sheep, and its flesh is excellent. The bandicoot is a repulsive animal, a foot and a-half long, which would give lessons in pillaging farm-yards to a European fox. Paganel killed it, and thought it charming. Amongst other large game Robert skilfully brought down a "dasyure viverrin," a sort of small fox with black fur spotted with white, and a couple of opossums, who were hiding in the thick foliage of the large trees.

But the kangaroo hunt was the most interesting part of the proceedings. The dogs, about four p.m., started a band of these curious animals; the young re-entered the maternal pouch in precipitation, and they all ran off in single file. Their hind legs are twice as long as their fore legs, and they bound as if set in motion by a spring. At the head of the flying herd was a male, at least five feet high, a magnificent specimen of the "macropus giganteus," an "old man," as the bushmen say. The hunters gave them chase for four or five miles, and the dogs, who were afraid, and not without reason, of their vigorous paws, armed with a sharp claw, did not care to approach them. But at last the exhausted herd stopped, and the "old man" leant against a tree trunk ready to defend himself. One of the pointers sprang at him, and a minute afterwards fell back dead. The entire pack would not have got the better of these powerful creatures; bullets alone could bring them down. At that moment Robert almost fell a victim to his imprudence. In order to get a good aim he went so near the kangaroo that the animal sprang upon him. Mary Grant, from the break, stretched out her hands in terror towards her young brother. Suddenly John Mangles took out his hunting-knife, threw himself on the kangaroo, and struck the animal in the heart. Robert was uninjured; in another minute he was in his sister's arms.

This incident terminated the hunt. The kangaroos had dispersed after the death of their chief, whose remains were carried to the house. It was then six o'clock in the evening, and a magnificent dinner awaited the sportsmen. Amongst other dishes a kangaroo-tail soup, prepared in the native manner, was much appreciated. After dessert the guests went to the drawing-room, and the evening was consecrated to music. Lady Glenarvan was a very good pianist, and put her talents at the disposition of the squatters. Michael and Sandy Patterson sang passages from the latest works of Gounod, Victor Massé, Félicien David, and even some of Wagner's " music of the future."

At eleven o'clock tea was brought in; it was made with that English perfection that no other nation can equal. But Paganel, having asked to taste Australian tea, they brought him a liquid as black as ink—a quart of water in which half a pound of tea had been boiled for four hours. Paganel declared it was excellent, notwithstanding his grimaces. At midnight the guests were shown to their cool and comfortable rooms, where they continued the pleasures of the day in their dream.

At daybreak the next morning they took leave of the young squatters, with many thanks and promises to meet again in Europe, at Malcolm Castle. Then the waggon set out, turned round the base of Mount Hottam, and soon the habitation disappeared like a rapid vision. Their way lay over station soil for five miles more, and it was not until nine o'clock that they passed the east palisade, and the little troop were in the almost unknown districts of Victoria.

CHAPTER XVI.

THE AUSTRALIAN ALPS.

N immense barrier closed the route on the south-east. It was the chain of the Australian Alps, which stretch over a length of fifteen miles, and rise 4000 feet in the air.

John Mangles and his two sailors went on in front to choose the practicable passes, and often to cut the way through a thicket of shrubs. Though Ayrton was so good a driver, he could not always prevent the waggon getting a jolt, which the ladies took in very good part. It took all the strength of the oxen to draw along the damp and clayey soil. They scarcely cleared half a degree that day, and encamped at the foot of the Alps, on the banks of the Cobongra Creek, in a little plain covered with shrubs four feet high, with light-red leaves.

"We shall have some difficulty in crossing those mountains," said Glenarvan, looking at their outline, already fading in the darkness. "Alps is a name that gives food for reflection."

"Do not imagine that we have a second Switzerland

before us," said Paganel. "In Australia there are the Grampians, Pyrenees, Alps, and Blue Mountains, as there are in Europe and America, but in miniature. It simply proves that the imagination of geographers is not infinite, or that the language of proper names is very poor."

"Then the Australian Alps——" began Helena.

"Are pocket mountains," answered Paganel. "We shall cross them before we are aware of it."

"Speak for yourself," said the major. "It is only an absent-minded man like you who could cross a chain of mountains before being aware of it."

"Absent-minded!" cried Paganel. "But I am that no longer. I appeal to the ladies. Since I have set foot on this continent, have I not kept my promise? Have I made a single mistake?"

"No, Mr. Paganel," said Mary Grant; "you are now the most perfect of men."

"Too perfect," added Lady Glenarvan, laughing. "Your mistakes suited you."

"I think they did," answered Paganel. "If I make no more I shall be a man like any other. I hope before long to do something outrageous that will make you all laugh. When I don't make a mistake I seem to have missed my vocation."

The next day, the 9th of January, notwithstanding the assurances of the confident geographer, it was not without great difficulty that the little troop began the ascent of the Alps. They were obliged to go at random along deep and narrow gorges, which might have no egress. Ayrton would, doubtless, have been much embarrassed if, after an hour's march, an inn, a miserable "tap," had not appeared on one of the mountain paths.

"The landlord can't make much of a fortune here," cried Paganel. "What can it·be used for?"

"To give us the information we want about our route," answered Glenarvan. "Let us enter."

Glenarvan, followed by Ayrton, crossed the threshold of the Bush Inn, and saw the landlord, a rough fellow, whose face indicated that he was his own best customer for brandy, whiskey, and gin. Generally he saw no one but squatters and cattle dealers. His answers, given in a bad-tempered tone, to the questions Ayrton asked him, indicated the proper route. Glenarvan indemnified the landlord for his trouble, and was going to leave the tavern, when a bill pasted on the wall caught his attention. It was a Colonial police notice about the escape of the convicts from Perth, and setting a price on the head of Ben Joyce. It offered £100 to whoever would give him up.

"Decidedly," said Glenarvan to the quartermaster, "that wretch deserves hanging."

"He is not worth the hundred pounds set on his head," answered Ayrton.

"I do not like the appearance of the tavern-keeper," said Glenarvan, "notwithstanding his police notice."

"Nor I either," answered Ayrton.

Glenarvan and the quartermaster rejoined the waggon, which immediately started for the point where the Lucknow Road stops. There a narrow path began to wind round the chain, and they commenced the ascent. They were often obliged to dismount to help the heavy waggon along, or hold it back in perilous declivities. Ayrton was obliged to harness the horses to the waggon to help the oxen, though it was as much as the poor animals could do to climb themselves.

Either from the prolonged fatigue or some other unknown cause one of the horses succumbed that day. It
dropped down suddenly. It was Mulrady's horse, and
when he tried to get it up he found it was dead.
Ayrton examined the animal, and seemed unable to
understand its sudden death.

"It must have broken some blood-vessel," said
the major.

"Evidently," answered Paganel.

"Take my horse, Mulrady," said Glenarvan. "I
will get into the waggon."

Mulrady obeyed, and the little troop continued its
fatiguing ascension, leaving the horse's body to the
ravens.

The chain of the Australian Alps is not very wide,
its base only covers a width of eight miles. If, therefore, the passage chosen by Ayrton led to the eastern
slope, it ought only to take forty-eight hours to cross
the mountain. Once the mountains crossed, the road
would be level and easy to the sea.

During the day of the 18th the travellers attained
the highest point of the Pass, about 2,000 feet up.
They were then on a plateau from which there
stretched a distant view. Towards the north sparkled
the waters of Lake Omeo, covered with water birds,
and beyond it lay the vast plains of the Murray.
On the south stretched the verdant plains of Gipps-
land, sheltered behind the screen of mountains, their
farthest limits lost in obscurity, as though night had
already received them in her arms. This contrast
was felt by the spectators, placed between two such
different scenes, and they did not look without
emotion at the almost unknown country which

they were going to cross to get to the frontiers of
Victoria.

They encamped on the plateau, and the next day
began the descent. It was steep, and made more difficult by a storm of hail which assailed the travellers,
and forced them to take refuge under the rocks. The
hailstones were great panes of ice as large as the hand.
The tarpaulin of the waggon was torn by them in
several places, and Paganel's scientific ardour was
quenched in bruises. The hailstorm delayed the
travellers about an hour, and when they again set out
the roads were still slippery.

Towards evening the waggon, disjointed in several
places, but still solid on its wooden wheels, was
descending the east slopes of the Alps amongst large
and isolated pine-trees. The chain had been crossed
without accident, and the usual arrangements were
made for the evening encampment.

The next morning Ayrton pressed Lord Glenarvan to
send the order for the Duncan to join him on the coast.
He wished Glenarvan to profit by the Lucknow road
to Melbourne. If he waited any longer it would be
difficult, for there would be no direct communication
with the capital. These recommendations of the
quartermaster seemed good, and Paganel advised
Glenarvan to follow them. Glenarvan was undecided,
especially as the major was quite opposed to continuing
the journey without Ayrton, as they did not know the
route, and the quartermaster alone could show them
the exact spot where the Britannia was wrecked. John
Mangles was of the same opinion as MacNabbs; and
the young captain observed that Glenarvan's orders
would reach the Duncan more easily if sent from Two-

fold Bay than by a messenger, who would have to cross 200 miles of wild country. The latter course was adopted, and the major noticed Ayrton's disappointment, but said nothing about his observation.

The plains which stretched from the foot of the Australian Alps were level, with a slight slope towards the east. Thickets of mimosas and eucalyptus, different gum-trees, broke the monotonous uniformity. The "gastrolobium grandiflorum" made the ground bristle with its bright flowering shrubs. From twelve o'clock till two they were crossing a curious forest of ferns, which were so high that horses and riders passed under their leaves. Paganel sighed with satisfaction at the delightful shade they gave. He was expatiating on the satisfaction it gave him when all at once his companions saw him shake on his horse, and both horse and rider fall in an inert mass. Was it a sudden giddiness, or worse, a suffocation, caused by the heat? They ran to him, and Glenarvan cried—

"Paganel! Paganel! What is the matter?"

"The matter is, I have no horse left," answered Paganel, getting out of the stirrups.

"What has come to him?"

"He is dead, as suddenly as Mulrady's."

Glenarvan, John Mangles, and Wilson examined the animal. It was quite dead.

"This is very singular," said John Mangles.

"Yes, very singular," murmured the major.

Glenarvan was much preoccupied with this fresh accident. If his horses were struck with an epidemic he should be much embarrassed to continue his route.

Before the end of the day the word "epidemic"

seemed justified. A third horse, Wilson's, fell dead, and one of the oxen also succumbed. The means of transport were reduced to three oxen and four horses.

The situation became grave. The dismounted men could, if necessary, go on foot. Many squatters had walked across these desert regions. But if they were obliged to abandon the waggon, what would become of the ladies? How could they accomplish the 120 miles that still separated them from Twofold Bay?

John Mangles and Glenarvan attentively examined the surviving horses, and could find no symptom of illness, or even weakness, amongst them; they hoped that the singular epidemic would make no more victims. Ayrton could not understand the misfortune.

They set out again, and the pedestrians took it in turns to have a lift in the waggon. In the evening, after a march of ten miles only, the encampment was organised, and the night was passed under a thicket of arborescent ferns, amongst which flew enormous bats, justly named flying foxes.

The next day, the 13th of January, no accident of the same nature happened again. The health of the travellers continued good. Horses and oxen did their work well. Lady Glenarvan's receptions were very animated, thanks to the number of visits she received. Mr. Olbinett took care to circulate refreshments that 30° of heat rendered necessary. Half a barrel of Scotch ale was entirely consumed, and they declared Barclay and Co. the greatest men of Great Britain.

A day so well begun ought to end well, too. They had cleared fifteen good miles along an undulated country, and hoped to encamp the same evening on the banks of the Snowy, an important river which flows

into the Pacific at the south of Victoria. In the evening
a mist on the horizon marked the course of the Snowy.
A forest of high trees was perceived at a turning in the
route behind a slight rise in the ground. Ayrton drove
his team through the wood; he had passed it, and was
half a mile from the river, when suddenly the wheels of
the waggon sank half way up in the mud.

"Look out!" called he to the men on horseback who
were following him.

"What is it?" asked Glenarvan.

"We are stuck in the mud," answered Ayrton.

He incited his oxen with his voice and goad, but they
only sank deeper in their struggles to get free.

"We must encamp here," said John Mangles.

"That is the best thing we can do," answered Ayrton.
"To-morrow we can see to get out of this."

Glenarvan gave orders to halt. Night had succeeded
a very short twilight, but heat had not gone with the
sun. The atmosphere was stifling, and lightning flashes
at intervals told of some distant storm.

Ayrton succeeded, after a great deal of trouble, in
getting his three oxen out of the mud, where they were
embedded up to their flanks. The quartermaster saw
to their forage and that of the horses; Glenarvan
remarked that he was particularly careful about it then,
and was glad to, see it, for the good condition of the
team was of the greatest importance.

After supper, Lady Glenarvan and Mary Grant retired to the waggon, whilst the men slept, some under
the tent, and others on the thick grass under the trees,
which in that healthy country is not attended with
unpleasant consequences.

By degrees they all fell into a heavy sleep. The

darkness grew greater under a curtain of thick clouds that covered the sky. There was not a breath of wind in the atmosphere. The silence of night was only interrupted by that "minor third" of the "morepork" which the poet Browning wrongly asserts "none but the cuckoo knows."

About eleven o'clock, after a heavy and fatiguing sleep, the major awoke. His half-shut eyes perceived an indistinct light moving amongst the trees. He got up, walked towards it, and was greatly surprised to find himself in presence of a remarkable natural phenomenon. Under his eyes extended an immense field of fungi, which emitted phosphorescent light. The major was going to awaken Paganel, that he might see it too, when an incident stopped him. The phosphorescent light illuminated the wood for the space of half a mile, and MacNabbs thought he saw some shadows pass rapidly across the lighted edge. He lay down, and, after a rigorous observation, distinctly perceived several men looking on the ground at some still fresh footprints. He was determined to know what they were doing, and, without awakening his companions, he crawled along the ground like a savage of the prairies, and disappeared under the tall grass.

CHAPTER XVII.

AN UNFORESEEN EVENT.

IT was a frightful night. At two p.m. the rain began to fall in torrents, and the tent became an insufficient shelter. Glenarvan and his companions took refuge in the waggon, but they could not sleep. They talked, and the major, whose short absence had not been remarked, was the only one who kept silence. The rain did not leave off, and they feared the Snowy would overflow, which, with a waggon already stuck fast in the mud, would have much increased the difficulties of their position. Mulrady, Ayrton, and John Mangles went out several times to examine the level of the running water, and came back wet through.

At last daylight appeared. The rain ceased, but the sunlight could not pierce the thick clouds. Large puddles of yellowish water, almost as large as ponds, covered the soil.

Glenarvan occupied himself with the waggon first of all. He found it was stuck in the loam, in the midst of a vast depression in the ground. It would take the united strength of oxen, horses, and men to clear the heavy machine.

"We must make haste," said John Mangles; "this loam will dry up, and make the operation more difficult."

Glenarvan, his two sailors, John Mangles, and Ayrton went into the wood to fetch the animals, but their astonishment was great at not finding them where they were left the night before. With their clogs on

K

they could not go far. They searched the wood without finding them, and Ayrton, surprised, then returned to the bank of the Snowy, bordered with magnificent mimosas. He called to his team, but they did not appear as usual at his voice. The quartermaster seemed very uneasy, and his companions looked at one another in disappointment.

An hour was passed in a vain search, and Glenarvan was going back to the waggon, from whence he was a good mile distant, when he heard a neighing and bellowing.

" They are there!" cried Mangles, gliding amongst the tufts of " gastrolobium," which were high enough to hide a herd of cattle. Glenarvan, Mulrady, and Ayrton followed him, and saw three horses and two oxen lying dead upon the ground, while a flock of thin ravens were croaking in the mimosas, watching their unexpected prey. The four men looked at each other, and Wilson could not restrain an oath that came up in his throat.

" Hush, Wilson," said Glenarvan, hardly containing himself, " we cannot help it. Ayrton, take back the ox and horse that remain, we must do with them."

" If the waggon were not embedded, these two animals would suffice to draw it to the coast by short stages. We must get the waggon out at any price."

" We will try, John," answered Glenarvan. " Now we must go back, or they will be uneasy at our prolonged absence."

Ayrton led the ox and Mulrady the horse, and they returned by the winding river paths. Half an hour after they all knew about the unfortunate event. The major had kept silence very well till then, but now he could not help saying—

"It is a pity all the horses did not want shoeing after crossing the Wimerra?"

"Why, sir?" asked Ayrton.

"Because the only horse left is the one you had shod there!"

"So it is," said John Mangles. "That's very singular."

"Yes, it is," said the quartermaster, looking fixedly at the major.

MacNabbs bit his lips to prevent himself speaking. Glenarvan, Mangles, and Helena wanted to hear him explain his allusion, but he said nothing, and walked towards the waggon, which Ayrton was examining.

"What did he mean?" said Glenarvan to the young captain.

"I don't know," he answered. "The major is not a man to speak without a reason."

"No, he is not," said Helena. "It looks as if he suspected Ayrton."

"What of?" said Paganel, shrugging his shoulders.

"He cannot suspect him of killing our oxen and horses," said Glenarvan. "He can have no interest in doing so."

"But still I should like to know what the major meant," said Mangles.

"Do you think he suspects him of acting in concert with the convicts?" said Paganel, imprudently.

"What convicts?" asked Mary.

"Mr. Paganel is making a mistake," answered John Mangles, quickly. "He knows there are no convicts in Victoria."

"Of course; what was I saying!" cried Paganel. "Who has ever heard of convicts in Australia? The climate, you know, Miss Mary——"

The poor savant, wishing to repair his error, did like the waggon—stuck in the mud. Lady Glenarvan was looking at him, and it embarrassed him exceedingly, seeing which Helena drew Mary to the other side of the tent where Olbinett was preparing the dinner according to all the rules of the culinary art.

"I deserve transporting," said Paganel, piteously.

"I think so," answered Glenarvan, so seriously that the poor savant was overwhelmed.

Glenarvan and Mangles went towards the waggon, where Ayrton and the two sailors were trying to get it free. The ox and horse, harnessed side by side, were pulling with all the strength of their muscles. Wilson and Mulrady were pushing the wheels, while the quartermaster, with whip and goad, excited his ill-matched team. The heavy vehicle did not stir. The loam, dry already, held it down fast. Mangles had the loam watered to make it less tenacious. It was in vain. The waggon did not move. After a few more vigorous efforts, animals and men stopped. Unless they were willing to take the machine to pieces, they must give up the hope of getting it free. They could not do that without proper tools. Ayrton was going to make a fresh effort, when Glenarvan stopped him.

"That is enough, Ayrton," said he. "We must take care of the only animals we have left. If we must continue our route on foot, one can carry the ladies and the other the provisions."

"Very well, my lord," answered Ayrton, taking the two animals out of the shafts.

"Now, we must decide what to do next," said Glenarvan. "We will go back to the tent and consult the others."

After a tolerably good breakfast the subject was mooted, and all were called upon to give their opinion. The first thing to do was to ascertain the position of the encampment. Paganel found they were on the 37th parallel, in longitude 147° 53', on the banks of the Snowy River.

"What is the exact longitude of Twofold Bay?" asked Glenarvan.

"A hundred and fifty degrees," answered Paganel.

"That makes seventy-five miles. How far is Melbourne from here?"

"Two hundred miles, at least."

"Now we know where we are," said Glenarvan, "what must be done?"

The answer was unanimous to go to the coast at once. Lady Glenarvan and Mary Grant said they could easily walk five miles a day. The courageous women were not alarmed at the idea of going all the distance on foot.

"You are a valiant companion for a traveller," said Glenarvan to his wife. "We are certain to find all the resources we need when we get to Eden."

"There is no doubt about that," said Paganel. "Eden has already been some years in existence, and must have frequent communication with Melbourne. I should think we can revictual at Delegete, on the frontier of Victoria, and find means of transport there, too."

"Don't you think it would be well to send word from here to the Duncan to meet you at the Bay?" asked Ayrton.

"What do you think, John?" asked Glenarvan.

"I do not think there is any need to hurry, my lord," said the young captain; "it will be always time to send to the Duncan. It will only take us four or five days to get to Eden."

"Four or five days!" exclaimed Ayrton; "say fifteen or twenty, and you will be nearer the mark."

"Fifteen or twenty days to go seventy-five miles!" cried Glenarvan.

"At least, my lord. You will have to cross the most difficult part of Victoria, nothing but bush, where you will often have to cut your own path."

Ayrton had spoken in a firm voice. Paganel approved of all the quartermaster had said.

"I admit the difficulty," said Mangles. "In a fortnight, then, your lordship can send your orders to Tom Austin."

"I must add," continued Ayrton, "that the principal obstacle is the Snowy, and you will very likely have to wait till the water goes down."

"To wait!" exclaimed Mangles. "Is there no ford, then?"

"I do not think so," answered Ayrton. "This morning I looked for one in vain. It is rare to meet with so rapid a river at this epoch."

"Is the Snowy wide, then?" asked Lady Glenarvan.

"Both wide and deep, your ladyship; it is a mile in width, and the current is great; a good swimmer would not cross it without danger."

"Well, we must build a raft," cried Robert, "or a canoe. There are plenty of trees here."

"Robert is right," said Mangles. "That is what

we shall have to do. It is useless to lose any more time in talking."

"What do you think about it, Ayrton?" asked Glenarvan.

"I think, my lord, that unless some help comes, a month hence will still find us on the banks of the Snowy."

"Have you any better plan?" asked Mangles, impatiently.

"Yes, if the Duncan comes to Twofold Bay."

"You are always talking about the Duncan; how could she help us?"

Ayrton hesitated a few minutes before he answered, and then said, evasively—

"I don't want you to follow my advice. I am quite ready to set out when his lordship gives the order" Then he crossed his arms.

"That is no answer, Ayrton," replied Glenarvan. "Tell us your plan."

"I propose that we do not go any farther without conveyance. We must wait for help here, and that help can only come from the Duncan. We could wait here while one of us takes the order to Tom Austin."

This proposition was received with surprise by the majority, and John Mangles did not conceal his antipathy to it.

"During that time," said Ayrton, "the Snowy will go down, and you can find a practicable ford or build a canoe. That is my plan, my lord."

"Very well, Ayrton," answered Glenarvan; "your plan deserves to be taken into serious consideration. The great objection to it is the delay it would cause, but it would save much fatigue and, perhaps, real danger."

"What do you think, cousin?" said Helena. "You have said nothing."

"Ayrton's advice seems the best to me, and I am of his opinion," answered MacNabbs.

No one expected this answer, for until then MacNabbs had always spoken against Ayrton. The quartermaster seemed surprised, and gave the major a rapid glance. Paganel, Lady Glenarvan, and the sailors were much disposed to vote for Ayrton's plan, and they hesitated no longer after MacNabbs had spoken thus. Glenarvan, therefore, declared Ayrton's plan adopted in principle.

"Now, John," added he, "do you not think prudence commands us to encamp here, and wait for means of conveyance?"

"Yes," answered Mangles, "if your messenger succeeds in crossing the Snowy, which we cannot cross ourselves."

They all looked at the quartermaster, who smiled with an air of self-confidence.

"The messenger will not cross the river," said he.

"Ah!" exclaimed John Mangles.

"He will simply go back to the Lucknow road, which will take him direct to Melbourne."

"Then he must go two hundred and fifty miles on foot!" cried the young captain.

"On horseback," replied Ayrton. "There is one good horse left. It will take four days. Add two for the Duncan to get to the Bay, and in one week the messenger will be back with what is required."

The major approved these words of Ayrton's with a

gesture which astonished John Mangles greatly. They had all voted for the quartermaster's plan, and the only thing to do now was to put it in execution.

"Now we must choose our messenger," said Glenarvan. "Who will go?"

Wilson, Mulrady, John Mangles, Paganel, and even Robert, offered themselves immediately. John insisted upon being allowed to go. But Ayrton said—

"I think your lordship had better send me. I am accustomed to the country. Many a time have I crossed more difficult regions. I can manage where another person would find himself in a fix. Give me a word for your second, and in six days the Duncan shall be at Twofold Bay."

"Well said," answered Glenarvan. "You are an intelligent fellow, Ayrton, and you will succeed."

It was evident that the quartermaster was the fittest messenger. They all saw that, and withdrew in his favour. John Mangles made a last objection, saying that Ayrton's presence was necessary to find traces of the Britannia. But the major observed that, as they were going to stop on the banks of the Snowy till Ayrton's return, there was no question of renewing the search without him.

"Very well; then go, Ayrton," said Glenarvan. "Go, and come back as quickly as you can."

A flash of satisfaction shone in the eyes of the quartermaster. He turned away his head, but not quickly enough to prevent John Mangles seeing the flash, which increased his suspicions of Ayrton.

The quartermaster made his preparations for departure, helped by the two sailors, one seeing to his horse and the other to his provisions. During that time

Glenarvan wrote the letter to Tom Austin, in which he ordered him to take the Duncan to Twofold Bay. He recommended the quartermaster to him as a man worthy of all confidence.

MacNabbs, who was looking over Glenarvan's shoulder, stopped him in the middle and asked him how he spelled Ayrton's name.

"As it is pronounced, of course," answered Glenarvan.

"You are wrong," answered the major, calmly. "It is pronounced Ayrton, but it is written Ben Joyce!"

———

CHAPTER XVIII.

ALAND ZEALAND.

HE revelation of this name of Ben Joyce produced the effect of a thunderclap. Ayrton started up suddenly, with a revolver in his hand. A report was heard, and Glenarvan fell, struck by a bullet. Shots were also heard outside.

John Mangles and the sailors rushed to seize Ben Joyce, but the audacious convict was too quick for them, and escaped to his band, who were waiting for him on the borders of the wood.

The tent was not a sufficient protection from the bullets. They were obliged to beat a retreat. Glenarvan, only slightly wounded, had got up.

"We must get to the waggon!" exclaimed John Mangles; and he dragged Lady Glenarvan and Mary Grant to their place of safety behind the thick leather curtains of their compartment. They were soon followed by the rest, and all the men stood, rifle in hand, awaiting the assault of the convicts. These events had happened with the rapidity of lightning. John Mangles attentively watched the edge of the wood. The shots had suddenly ceased on the arrival of Ben Joyce. Some white smoke still curled amongst the branches of the gum-trees. All other indication of the convicts' presence had vanished.

The major and John Mangles went as far as the wood to reconnoitre. The place was deserted. There were numerous footprints on the ground, but no other traces of the convicts.

" They have gone away," said Mangles.

" Yes," answered the major; "and their disappearance makes me uneasy. I prefer to meet them face to face. A tiger in the plain is better than a serpent in the grass."

They did not return to the waggon till they had searched all the ground in its neighbourhood. Ben Joyce's band seemed to have taken flight like a flock of birds of prey. This disappearance was too singular to leave the travellers in perfect security, and they resolved to keep a sharp look-out. The waggon became a fortress, and two men, relieved every hour, were stationed on guard.

The first care of Lady Glenarvan and Mary Grant had been to dress Lord Glenarvan's wound. The bullet had merely grazed his shoulder, and though it bled a good deal, yet he was able to move his fingers and bend his elbow to convince his friends that he was uninjured. When his arm was dressed he would not let them pay any more attention to him and asked his companions what they knew about the affair.

The travellers, with the exception of Wilson and Mulrady, were then all in the waggon. The major told Lady Glenarvan about the escaped convicts and their crime on the railway, showing her the copy of the *Australian and New Zealand Gazette*, and saying how he had instinctively suspected Ayrton from the first. Two or three almost insignificant facts—a glance exchanged between the quartermaster and the farrier at the Wimerra river; Ayrton's evident dislike to entering a town or hamlet; his insistance about the Duncan; the strange death of the animals confided to his care; in short, a want of openness about him, had all awakened the major's suspicions. He could not, however, have accused him directly but for the events of the preceding night, which have already been related. When he had arrived near the suspected shadows by crawling through the grass, he saw, by the light of the phosphorescent plants, that there were three men examining footprints recently made, and amongst them the farrier of Black Point. They were talking about the peculiar shape of one of the horse's footprints, which convinced them they were on the right track.

" All the other horses are dead now," said he.

" Yes," said another, " there is enough gastrolobium about to poison a regiment of cavalry."

" Then," added MacNabbs, " they went away, and I followed them. They soon began to talk again. ' That Ben Joyce is a brick,' said one; ' if Ayrton's plan succeeds, he will prove himself a famous quartermaster, I know.' At that moment the rascals left the wood. I knew all I wanted to, and came back to the encampment with the certainty that all convicts do not get reformed in Australia, notwithstanding Paganel."

When the major had finished speaking, his companions were silent for some time.

"Then," said Glenarvan, pale with anger, "Ayrton has brought us as far as here to be pillaged and massacred!"

"Yes," answered the major.

"And his band has been on our track ever since the Wimerra, waiting for a favourable occasion?"

"Yes."

"Then the wretch was no sailor from the Britannia at all?"

"Yes, I think he was," answered the major. "I believe his name really is Ayrton, and Ben Joyce is his alias. It is certain that he knew Captain Grant, and was quartermaster on board the Britannia."

"Then how do you explain the fact of Captain Grant's quartermaster being in Australia?" asked Glenarvan.

"I cannot explain it at all, nor the police either, it seems," said the major. "It is a mystery that the future may explain."

"The police do not even know that Ayrton and Ben Joyce are one and the same person," said Mangles.

"He must have introduced himself into the Irishman's farm with a criminal intention," said Lady Glenarvan.

"There is no doubt about it," answered MacNabbs. "He was premeditating some treachery there when a better opportunity turned up."

The conversation was interrupted by John Mangles, who, as usual, had been looking at Mary Grant, and had said—

"How pale you are, Miss Mary. Is anything the matter with you?"

"You are crying, my child," said Lady Glenarvan, whose attention was thus attracted to the young girl.

"My father!" were the only words the young girl could utter.

She could not go on, but they all understood why the tears came and she uttered her father's name. The discovery of Ayrton's treason took away all hope. The convict had invented the shipwreck to decoy Glenarvan. The Britannia had never been wrecked on the breakers of Twofold Bay, nor had Captain Grant ever set foot on the Australian continent! For the second time an erroneous interpretation of the document had put them on a false scent. The children's grief was touching, and Paganel was in despair.

In the meantime Glenarvan had gone out to Wilson and Mulrady, who were on guard. A deep silence reigned over the plain between the wood and the river. The clouds were very low, and in the profound torpor of the atmosphere the least sound would have been heard. Ben Joyce and his band must have retired to a considerable distance, for the flocks of birds had again settled down on the branches of the gum-trees, and kangaroos were feeding amongst the bushes, evident proof that there were no human beings in the immediate vicinity.

"Have you seen or heard anything since your watch began?" asked Glenarvan of his two sailors.

"No, your lordship," answered Wilson. "The convicts must be some miles from here."

"They cannot be in sufficient numbers to attack us," added Mulrady. "Ben Joyce is very likely gone to recruit his ranks amongst the bushrangers who wander about the foot of the Alps."

"Very likely, Mulrady," answered Glenarvan. "They are cowards, and know we are well armed. Perhaps they are waiting till night to attack us, and we must keep a good look out till morning. How I wish we could cross the Snowy, and continue our route eastwards."

"Why does not your lordship give us orders to build a raft?" said Wilson. "There is plenty of wood here."

"No, Wilson," answered Glenarvan. "The river is too rapid for any raft."

At that moment John Mangles, the major, and Paganel joined Glenarvan; they came to examine the state of the river. The waters, swelled by the recent rain, had risen another foot. They rushed along in an impetuous torrent like the American rapids. John Mangles declared it was impossible to cross.

"But," added he, "we must not remain here without attempting anything. What you were going to do before Ayrton's treason is still more necessary now."

"What do you mean, John?" asked Glenarvan.

"I mean that it is urgent to seek help; and as you cannot get to Twofold Bay, some one must go to Melbourne. There is one horse left, let me take it and go."

"But that is a dangerous experiment," said Glenarvan, "not only because Melbourne is 200 miles from here, but because Ben Joyce and his comrades are sure to guard the road."

"I know it, my lord; but I know, too, that our present position must not be prolonged. Ayrton only

asked for a week's absence to return with the crew of
the Duncan, and I only ask for six days to do the same
thing. Your lordship has only to command."

"Before Lord Glenarvan decides," said Paganel, "1
have an observation to make. It is clear that some
one must go to Melbourne, but it must not be the captain of the Duncan. His life is too precious to be
risked so. I shall go instead."

"And why should it be you, pray ?" said the major.

"Are we not here ?" cried Mulrady and Wilson.

"And do you think I am afraid of two hundred
miles on horseback ?" said the major.

"We must draw lots," said Glenarvan.

"Will you write our names, Paganel ?"

"Not yours, my lord," said John Mangles.

"Why not ?" asked Glenarvan.

"You cannot leave Lady Glenarvan, especially as
your wound has not closed yet."

"Glenarvan," said Paganel, "you cannot leave the
expedition."

"No," replied the major, "your place is here,
Edward."

"There are risks to be run," answered Glenarvan,
"and I am not going to put my share on to other
people. Write my name too, Paganel, and Heaven
grant it may be the first to come out."

They were obliged to obey him. Glenarvan's name
was added to the others. The lot fell to Mulrady, and
the brave sailor uttered an hurrah of satisfaction.

"I am ready to start, my lord," said he.

Glenarvan shook hands with him, and then returned
to the waggon, leaving the major and John Mangles on
guard.

Lady Glenarvan was immediately informed of the intention to send a messenger to Melbourne, and to whose lot it had fallen to go. She spoke words to Mulrady that went to the heart of the brave sailor. They knew he was courageous, intelligent, and strong; the lot could not have fallen better. His departure was fixed for eight o'clock, after the short evening twilight. Wilson harnessed the horse, and changed the shoe put on at Black Point for another he took from one of the dead horses during the night. The convicts would not be able to recognise Mulrady's track nor follow him, as they had no horses.

Whilst Wilson was occupying himself with these details, Glenarvan prepared the letter for Tom Austin; but his wounded arm prevented him writing it himself, and he asked Paganel to do it for him. During all this time the Frenchman had been thinking of nothing but his falsely interpreted document, and did not hear Glenarvan's request until he repeated it.

"I shall be very happy," said Paganel.

While he spoke he was mechanically preparing his memorandum book, from which he tore a blank page and waited, pencil in hand. Glenarvan began to dictate the following instructions :—

"Order to Tom Austin to set sail at once, and take the Duncan ——"

Paganel was finishing the last words when his eye fell upon the copy of the *Australian and New Zealand Gazette*, which was lying on the ground. The paper was folded, and only showed the last two syllables of its title. Paganel's pencil stopped, and he seemed to forget all about Glenarvan, his letter, and his dictation.

"Well, Paganel," said Glenarvan, "what is the matter?"

"Nothing!" answered Paganel, then sinking his voice he repeated, "*Aland! aland! aland!*"

He had risen and seized the paper. They all looked at him in astonishment, but all at once he dropped back into his chair, and said, calmly—

"Go on, Glenarvan."

Glenarvan finished dictating the order, which ran as follows:—

"Order to Tom Austin to set sail at once, and take the Duncan to the eastern coast of Australia."

"Australia?" said Paganel. "Oh, yes, Australia!"

Then he finished the letter, and passed it to Glenarvan to sign, who managed to write his name. The letter was folded and sealed, and Paganel, with a hand still trembling from emotion, wrote the address—

> "Mr. Tom Austin,
>> "Mate on board the yacht Duncan,
>>> "Melbourne."

Then he left the waggon, repeating the incomprehensible words—

"*Aland! aland! Zealand!*"

CHAPTER XIX.

FOUR DAYS' ANGUISH.

HE rest of the day passed without incident. All the preparations for Mulrady's departure were ended, and the brave sailor was happy to be able to give his laird this proof of his attachment.

Paganel had recovered his usual composure. His look indicated some grave pre-occupation, but he seemed determined to keep it a secret. He had, doubtless, very good reasons for this determination, as the major heard him repeat these words like a man struggling with himself—

"No, no; they would not believe me. Besides, what would be the good? It is too late."

This resolution taken, he occupied himself with tracing out Mulrady's route for him from his map. All the "tracks," or paths through the bush, ended in the Lucknow Road. This route goes straight down south to the coast, and then turns off suddenly in the direction of Melbourne. Mulrady would only have to keep to it rigorously.

The only danger lay near the encampment, where Ben Joyce and his band were in ambush. Once away, Mulrady was certain of out-distancing them, and fulfilling his important mission in safety.

At six o'clock the meal was taken in common. Torrents of rain were falling. The tent was not a sufficient shelter, and they had all taken refuge in the waggon, which was besides a safe retreat.

The night proved a very dark one, favourable for Mulrady's departure. They had tied up his horses' feet in linen, so that they should be noiseless, and John Mangles put a six-barrelled revolver into his hand, which he had just loaded with the greatest care. It would be a formidable weapon in the hands of a determined man, for six shots fired in a few seconds would clear a road obstructed by felons. Mulrady got into the saddle, they all shook him by the hand, and he soon disappeared along the edge of the wood. At that moment the wind redoubled its violence. It shook the high branches of the eucalyptus in its fury, and many a giant tree, whose sap was exhausted, fell during the tempest.

After Mulrady's departure, the travellers cowered together in the waggon. Lady Glenarvan, Mary Grant, Glenarvan, and Paganel occupied the front compartment, which had been hermetically closed. In the second, Olbinett, Wilson, and Robert had found sufficient shelter. The major and Mangles were on watch outside, an act of necessary prudence, for an attack was easy, and consequently possible. They tried to pierce the darkness, and listened to the roar of the wind. Sometimes it calmed for a few minutes, as if to take breath, and then the roar of the Snowy alone was distinguishable. It was during one of these intervals that the noise of a shrill whistle reached them. John Mangles went rapidly towards the major.

"Did you hear?" said he.

"Yes," said MacNabbs. "Was it a man or an animal?"

"A man," answered John Mangles. Then both listened. The inexplicable whistle was repeated, and something like a shot followed it, but the wind then began again, and they could not clearly distinguish the sound.

At that moment the curtains of the waggon were raised, and Glenarvan joined his two companions. He also had heard the whistle and the report that followed it.

"In what direction was it?" he asked.

"That!" said Mangles, pointing to the dark path taken by Mulrady.

"At what distance?"

"It came on the wind," answered Mangles, "and must have been at least three miles off."

"We must go towards it," said Glenarvan, throwing his rifle over his shoulder.

"You must not go!" answered the major. "It is a trap to decoy us from the waggon."

"But suppose it is a signal from Mulrady!" exclaimed Glenarvan, seizing the hand of MacNabbs.

"We shall know that to-morrow," said the major coldly, firmly resolved to prevent Glenarvan committing any useless imprudence.

"You cannot leave the encampment, my lord," said Mangles. "I will go alone."

"You shall not go either," said the major with energy. "Do you want them to kill us in detail? If Mulrady has been their victim it is a misfortune, and a second must not be added to it. If the lot had fallen to me instead of to Mulrady, I should have been in the same predicament, and should neither ask nor expect help."

Good as the major's reasoning was it did not convince Glenarvan, who came and went around the waggon a prey to feverish excitement. While the major was trying to persuade him to go in again a cry of distress was heard.

"Listen!" said Glenarvan.

The cry came in the same direction as the whistle, and seemed to be less than a quarter of a mile off. Glenarvan pushed the major aside, and was already on the path, when these words were heard at 300 paces from the waggon.

"Help! help!"

The voice seemed weak and desperate. John Mangles and the major rushed towards it. A few minutes after they perceived a human form crawling along the underwood and uttering fearful groans.

It was Mulrady, wounded and dying. When his companions raised him they felt their hands wet with his blood. Glenarvan came up and helped them to carry the wounded man to the waggon. On their arrival every one rose. Paganel, Robert, Wilson, and Olbinett left the waggon, and Lady Glenarvan gave up her compartment to the poor sailor. The major removed his vest and discovered the wound; it was a dagger-thrust in the right side. MacNabbs dressed it skilfully; he could not tell whether the weapon had reached any vital organ. The blood was flowing from the wound, and the major succeeded in stanching it. Mulrady was placed on his other side, with his head and shoulders well raised, and Lady Helena made him drink a little water.

In about a quarter of an hour the wounded man, who had been motionless till then, made a movement. He muttered incoherent words, and the major, bending down his ear, heard him say—

"My lord —— the letter —— Ben Joyce ——."

The major repeated these words, and looked at his companions. What did Mulrady want to say? Ben Joyce had attacked the sailor, but why? Was it only to stop him and prevent the arrival of the Duncan?

Glenarvan searched Mulrady's pockets for his letter to Tom Austin, but it was no longer there.

The night was passed in anxiety and misery. They feared the wounded man might die at any moment. He was devoured by fever. Lady Glenarvan and Mary Grant, two sisters of charity, never left him, and he had the most tender nursing.

Daylight came at last. The rain had ceased. Thick clouds were still moving across the sky. The ground was covered with wood from the trees. The loam, soaked by the rain, was again soft, and it became difficult to get to the waggon, but it could not sink any deeper.

John Mangles, Paganel, and Glenarvan went as soon as it was light to make a survey of the ground in the neighbourhood of the encampment. They went up the path to the place where Mulrady had been attacked. There two bodies lay on the ground killed by him. One was that of the farrier of Black Point. His face looked horrible in death.

Glenarvan did not extend his investigations any farther. He came back to the waggon absorbed by the gravity of his position.

"We cannot think of sending another messenger to Melbourne," said he.

"But we must, my lord," answered John Mangles. "You must let me go this time."

"No, John, you have not even a horse to carry you the two hundred miles."

In fact, Mulrady's horse, the only one left, had not reappeared. Glenarvan supposed that the convicts must have taken possession of it.

"Whatever happens," said he, "we must all remain together. We must wait till the Snowy sinks—a week, or a fortnight, if necessary. We shall then reach Twofold Bay by easy stages, and once there we can send orders to the Duncan by safer means."

"It is the only thing to be done," answered Paganel. "We are only thirty-five miles from Delegete, the first frontier town of New South Wales, and there we shall find some conveyance to take us to Twofold Bay. Once there we can telegraph to Melbourne."

As they returned to the encampment Robert ran to meet them, crying—

"He is better! he is better!"

"Yes, Edward," said Lady Glenarvan, "there is a favourable change."

"Where is MacNabbs?" asked Glenarvan.

"With him. Mulrady asked to speak to you or the major. When the major saw how weak he was, he tried to prevent him speaking, but Mulrady insisted so that he was obliged to give in."

The interview had lasted some minutes when Glenarvan came back. But there was nothing to do but to await the major's report.

Soon the curtains of the waggon were drawn aside, and the major reappeared. He found his friends at the foot of a gum-tree, where the tent had been pitched. His face looked grave and sorrowful, and they soon knew why.

On leaving the encampment, Mulrady followed one of the paths indicated by Paganel. He was going as fast as the darkness would let him, and, according to his own estimation, he had ridden about two miles when several men—five he believes—threw themselves at his horse's head. The animal reared. Mulrady seized his revolver and fired, and it seemed to him that two of his assailants fell. By the light of the explosion he recognised Ben Joyce, but that was all. He had not time to discharge his weapon. A violent blow on the right side brought him to the ground. However, he had not yet lost consciousness. The felons thought he was dead. He felt that they were searching him. Then he heard some one say—

" I have the letter."

" Give it to me," answered Ben Joyce. " Now the Duncan is ours !"

Here Glenarvan could not restrain a cry. MacNabbs went on—

" Now catch the horse," added Ben Joyce. " In two days I shall be on board the Duncan; in six at Twofold Bay. Cross the river at Kemple Pier, gain the coast, and wait for me there. I will find means to get you on board, and then, with a ship like the Duncan, we shall soon be masters of the Indian Ocean."

Then Ben Joyce mounted Mulrady's horse, and he disappeared along the Lucknow Road, whilst the band went south-east to the Snowy River. Although Mulrady was so grievously wounded, he had the strength to crawl to where we found him.

This revelation terrified Glenarvan and his companions.

"The Duncan a pirate ship!" cried Glenarvan. "My crew massacred!"

"Yes," said the major, "for Ben Joyce will reach the ship, and then——"

"We must reach the coast before the convicts!" said Paganel.

"But how are we to cross the Snowy?" asked Wilson.

"Like them," answered Glenarvan, "by Kemple Pier Bridge."

"But what is to become of Mulrady?" asked Lady Glenarvan.

"We must take it in turns to carry him. I cannot leave my crew to the mercy of Ben Joyce."

The idea of crossing the Snowy by Kemple Pier Bridge was practicable, but hazardous. The convicts might station themselves on the bridge and defend it. They would be at least thirty against seven. But there are moments when it is useless to count.

"My lord," then said Mangles, "before risking our last chance on this bridge, it would be prudent to go and reconnoitre. I will do that."

"I will accompany you, John," answered Paganel.

This proposition was accepted, and they set out at once. They were to go down the banks of the Snowy till they came to the bridge, and keep concealed from the convicts, who would probably be waiting about in the neighbourhood. They were well-armed, furnished with provisions, and they set out, hiding themselves amidst the tall reeds of the river.

Their companions expected them back all day. Evening came, and they had not returned, to the great anxiety of Glenarvan.

At last, about eleven p.m., Wilson saw them coming back, worn out with their ten miles' march.

"What about the bridge?" exclaimed Glenarvan rushing to meet them.

"It was there," said Paganel, "but the convicts have burnt it!"

CHAPTER XX.

EDEN.

IT was not the moment to despair, but to act. As Kemple Bridge Pier was destroyed, they must cross the Snowy at any cost, and get to Twofold Bay before the convicts. They lost no time in useless speech, and the next day, the 16th of January, John Mangles and Glenarvan went to look at the river. The water showed no symptom of going down, and it rushed along in a stormy torrent. It would be tempting death to try to cross it.

"Shall I try to swim across?" said John Mangles.

"No, John," answered Glenarvan, holding the young man back. "We must wait."

They both returned to the encampment, and the day passed in terrible anxiety. Glenarvan went backwards and forwards to the Snowy, and tried to imagine some plan for crossing it, but in vain. Had it been a torrent of lava, it would not have been more insuperable.

During these long hours of waiting, Lady Glenarvan, instructed by the major, nursed Mulrady with the most intelligent care. The sailor felt that he was returning to life, and MacNabbs could affirm that no vital organ had been injured. The loss of blood was sufficient to account for the invalid's extreme weakness. As soon as the wound closed up, his complete cure would be only a work of time. Lady Glenarvan had made him keep to her compartment of the waggon. Mulrady felt quite ashamed, and he was miserable at the idea that his state might delay Glenarvan, and they were obliged to promise that he should be left at the encampment, under the guard of Wilson, if it became practicable to cross the Snowy.

Unfortunately the passage was not possible either that day or the next, the 17th of January. Glenarvan grew desperate; his wife and the major tried in vain to calm and exhort him to patience. How could he be patient when, perhaps at that very moment, Ben Joyce was embarking on board his yacht, or every hour was bringing the Duncan nearer to the fatal coast?

John Mangles, wishing to overcome the obstacle at any price, built an Australian raft with large pieces of bark from the gum-trees, fastened together with logs of wood, and making but a fragile craft.

The captain and his sailor tried this frail canoe during the day of the 18th. All that skill, strength, and courage could do they did. But they were scarcely in the current when the boat capsized, and they were near paying their bold experiment with their lives. The boat, sucked in by the eddy, disappeared; they had not rowed twenty yards across a river a mile wide.

The two following days, the 19th and 20th, were lost in this position. The major and Glenarvan went five miles up the Snowy without finding a practicable passage. They were obliged to give up all hope of saving the Duncan. Five days had elapsed since the departure of Ben Joyce, time for the yacht to reach the coast, and be in the hands of the convicts. Still it was impossible to prolong this state of things. On the 21st Paganel found that the water had begun to sink and told Glenarvan so.

"What does it matter now?" answered Glenarvan; "it is too late!"

"That is no reason for stopping here," said the major.

"We shall very likely get rapid means of conveyance at Delegete," said Paganel, "and may arrive in time to prevent a misfortune."

"Then we will try it," cried Glenarvan.

John Mangles and Wilson immediately set about building another and a larger raft. Experience had taught them that bark was too light to withstand the current, so they made it of gum-tree trunks. It took some time, and was not finished till the next day. Then the Snowy had sunk perceptibly. The current was still strong, but John hoped to reach the opposite bank in safety.

They embarked at half-past twelve, taking with them as many provisions as they could carry for a two days' journey. The remainder was left with the waggon and the tent. Mulrady was well enough to go too, for his convalescence was rapid.

At one o'clock they were all on the raft. John Mangles had caused a sort of oar to be placed on the starboard, and entrusted it to Wilson, whilst he managed a rude helm he had made himself.

All went on well for about thirty yards, as Wilson managed to resist the current. But then the raft was caught in the eddy, and neither helm nor oar could keep

it straight. It began to float down stream with fearful
rapidity, and was dragged into the middle of the river.
John and Wilson, by means of their oars, managed to
make it take an oblique direction, and they neared the
left bank. They were not more than a hundred yards
from it when Wilson's oar broke, and the raft drifted
away again. John resisted the current with all his
might, and Wilson, with bleeding hands, joined his
efforts to those of his captain.

At last they succeeded, and after a passage that had
lasted more than half an hour, the raft struck on the left
bank. The shock was violent, the cords broke, and the
water bubbled in fast. The travellers had only time to
hold on to the overhanging bushes, and lift out Mulrady
and the two women, wet through; but the greater part
of the provisions and all the arms, with the exception
of the major's rifle, drifted away with the remains of
the raft.

The river was crossed, and the little troop was in a
desert country, thirty-five miles from Delegete, on the
frontier of Victoria. They would meet with neither
colonists nor squatters, for the whole region is uninhabited, except by ferocious and pillaging bushrangers.
They resolved to begin their journey at once, and Mulrady saw that he would be an incumbrance; he asked
to remain alone, and wait for succour from Delegete.
Glenarvan refused. He could not reach Delegete for
two days and the coast for five, which would bring
him to the 26th of January. The Duncan would have
left Melbourne on the 16th, so that a short delay would
make little difference.

"No," said he to Mulrady, "I will not leave you here.
We must make a litter, and carry you in turns."

The litter was constructed of eucalyptus branches covered with twigs, and Mulrady was placed upon it in spite of himself. Glenarvan wished to be the first to carry his sailor. He took one end of the litter and Wilson the other, and they thus continued their march.

This first day was passed silently and painfully They relieved each other in carrying the litter every ten minutes. None of the sailor's companions complained of this fatigue, though it was increased by the great heat.

In the evening, after a march of five miles only, they encamped under some gum-trees. The remainder of the provisions rescued from the raft furnished their evening meal. After that they had nothing to depend upon but the major's rifle. It rained during the night, and daylight seemed long in coming. They set out again at daybreak, but the major did not find occasion to fire one shot. The fatal desert seemed abandoned by animals as well as men.

Happily, Robert found a bustard's nest, in which were a dozen large eggs, which Olbinett cooked in cinders. The road then became extremely difficult. The sandy plains were bristling with "spinifex," a prickly plant which is called "porcupine" at Melbourne. It tore their garments and made their legs bleed. The courageous women did not complain, however; they walked along valiantly, setting the example and encouraging their companions with a look or a word.

They stopped in the evening at the foot of Mount Bulla-Bulla, on the banks of the Jungalla Creek. Their supper would have been a meagre one had not MacNabbs killed a large rat, the "mus conditor," which

is esteemed excellent food. Olbinett roasted it, and it
would have seemed worthy of even a greater reputation had it been as large as a sheep. As it was, there
was no meat left on the bones when they had done.

On the 23rd the tired but still energetic travellers
set out again. After having journeyed round the hill,
they marched over bush, the grass of which seemed
made of whalebone, and they were obliged to make a
road either with axe or fire.

That morning there was no question of breakfast,
and hunger and thirst were added to the difficulties of
walking over such ground on a burning day. They did
not walk half a mile an hour. If they had not at last
found means to slake their thirst, they could not have
gone much farther. They drank the contents of
"cephalots," a kind of cup filled with liquid that hung
from the branches of coralliform shrubs. Their food
was the same that keeps life in the natives when game,
insects, and serpents fail. Paganel discovered, in the
dried-up bed of a creek, a plant whose excellent qualities he had often heard described by one of his col-
leagues of the Geographical Society.

It was the "nardou," the same that prolonged the
life of Burke and King in the deserts of the interior.
Underneath its trefoil leaves grow dried sporules as
large as lentils. Crushed, they make a sort of bread
that appeases the tortures of hunger. There was a
great quantity of the plant in that place. Olbinett
made a large provision of it, and they had food assured
for several days.

The next day, the 24th, Mulrady went a part of the
way on foot. His wound was quite healed over. The
town of Delegete was only ten miles off when they

encamped in the evening at Delegete, in longitude 149°, on the frontier of New South Wales.

Fine and penetrating rain had been falling for some hours, and they would have to sleep shelterless but that John Mangles discovered a woodman's hut, abandoned and dilapidated. Wilson tried to light a fire in it to cook their nardou bread, and he went to pick up the dead wood that encumbered the ground. But when he tried to set fire to it the great quantity of aluminous matter it contained prevented it burning. It was the incombustible wood Paganel had cited in his nomenclature of Australian products.

They were obliged, therefore, to do without fire, and consequently without bread, and to sleep in their wet clothes, whilst the mocking birds, hidden in the high branches, seemed to scoff at these unfortunate travellers.

Glenarvan, however, was reaching the end of his troubles. It was time. The two young women made heroic efforts, but their strength failed hourly. They dragged themselves along, they could march no longer.

The next day they set out again at daybreak. At eleven a.m. Delegete appeared, in the county of Wellesley, fifty miles from Twofold Bay. Once there, the means of conveyance were rapidly organised. Hope returned to Glenarvan as he felt himself so near the coast. If there had been the least delay, he might arrive before the Duncan. In twenty-four hours he would reach the Bay.

At noon, after a comfortable meal, all the travellers were installed in a mail-coach, driven by five vigorous horses. The postilions, stimulated by the promise of a princely reward, kept the horses at a gallop, and did not lose two minutes at the relays every ten miles. It

M

seemed as if Glenarvan had communicated to them the ardour that devoured him.

All day and night they went on thus at a speed of six miles an hour.

The next day, at daybreak, a dull murmur announced the approach of the Indian Ocean. They were obliged to go round the Bay to reach the point on the 37th parallel where Tom Austin was to meet them.

When the sea appeared, all looks were turned towards it. Was the Duncan there by some miracle of Providence?

Nothing was to be seen. Sky and water mixed in the same horizon, and not a sail was to be seen on the vast expanse of ocean. One hope still remained. Perhaps Tom Austin had thought it prudent to drop anchor in Twofold Bay, for the sea was rough, and a ship could not ride in safety on the 37th parallel.

" To Eden !" said Glenarvan.

The mail-coach immediately turned to the right, and made for the small town of Eden, some five miles off.

The postilions stopped near the lights at the entrance to the port. A few ships were lying at anchor there, but the Duncan was not amongst them.

Glenarvan, John Mangles, and Paganel got down at the Custom House, where they questioned the clerks about the arrivals of the last few days. No ship had put into port there for the last week.

" Perhaps we have arrived first, and he did not start so soon," said Glenarvan.

John Mangles shook his head. He knew that Tom Austin would never have delayed the execution of an order so long as that. Glenarvan telegraphed to the shipbroker's office at Melbourne, and then the travellers were driven to the Victoria Hotel. At two p.m. a telegram was put into Lord Glenarvan's hand. It ran thus :—

> "To Lord Glenarvan,
> "Eden,
> "Twofold Bay.

"Duncan started on 18th instant. Destination unknown."

The telegram fell from Lord Glenarvan's hands.

There was no longer any doubt possible. The honest Scotch yacht, in the hands of Ben Joyce, had become a pirate ship.

Thus ended this journey across Australia begun under such favourable circumstances. All traces of Captain Grant seemed irrevocably lost. The search had cost the lives of a whole crew, and the courage which no natural event could damp had been exhausted by the perversity of man.